LETTERS FOR Emily

CAMRON WRIGHT

LETTERS *FOR* *Emily*

a novel

POCKET BOOKS

New York   London   Toronto   Sydney   Singapore

While the inspiration for this publication came from the life of my grandfather, this book is a work of fiction. Names, characters, places and incidents are products of the author's imagination or are used fictitiously. Any resemblance to actual events or locales or persons, living or dead, is entirely coincidental.

 POCKET BOOKS, a division of Simon & Schuster, Inc.
1230 Avenue of the Americas, New York, NY 10020

ISBN: 0-7434-4446-9

First Pocket Books hardcover printing January 2002

10 9 8 7 6 5 4 3 2 1

For information regarding special discounts for bulk purchases, please contact Simon & Schuster Special Sales at 1-800-456-6798 or business@simonandschuster.com

Jacket design by Lisa Litwack
Jacket photo © FPG International/Antony Nagelmann

Printed in the U.S.A.

To Alicyn,

Who believes in me, more than I believe in myself,

and

Nathan, Trevor, Danika, and Corbin

"See, when Dad's at the computer, he is working."

ACKNOWLEDGMENTS

I could not have finished this book without the help of many friends. From the heart, I thank the following:

Amanda Dickson of KSL Radio, the first person to call me a writer; her suggestions were always right on target. Dorian Karchmar, a fabulous agent who never skims; she not only has talent and tenacity, but also a sense of humor. Judith Curr, President and Publisher at Pocket Books; she recognized the potential through all of my mistakes and said, "Yes." Maggie Crawford, my extraordinary editor and advocate at Pocket Books, for her patience, guidance, and wisdom; she's a true professional. Karen Mender and Seale Ballenger, as well as the rest of the superb staff at Pocket Books; any success that this book achieves will be due in no small part to their efforts and creativity. *New York Times* bestselling author, James Pratt for lending his support. Screenwriter Ray Goldrup, for kind words of encouragement. Kathy Ashton, a wonderfully blunt editor who helped me get past the first revision. Earl Madsen, for seeing the vision from the beginning. My wife, Alicyn; she not only read the manuscript countless times, but she was always willing to listen. And to my grandfather, Harry S. Wright, for the memories that inspired the book.

CHAPTER *One*

MY BED IS FRIGID AND THE ROOM DARK. I'VE PLACED many blankets on my bed, but they don't stop the cold Wasatch wind that penetrates to my bones. I stare through the window at my snow-covered plants and realize I will miss my garden. I will miss the way the carrots emerge from seeds not much bigger than dust. I will miss thinning beets in the late spring. I will miss digging for new potatoes in the fall. I will miss harvesting buckets of zucchini for unsuspecting neighbors who will then have no idea what to do with them; and I will even miss watching the plants turn brown and die each year as winter sets in.

My garden has taught me that every living thing must die. I have watched it happen now for scores of years—I only wish I could have a few more summers in my garden with Emily.

I have other grandchildren, and I don't mean to play favorites, but the others live far away and seldom visit.

Emily visits with her mother every Friday. Though our ages are more than seven decades apart, Emily and I are best friends.

My name is Harry, a laughable name for a man who's been completely bald most of his life. But, hairy or not, it's my name nonetheless. It was my father's name before me, and his father's before him. I wish I could say it was a name I passed on to my own son. I can't. When he was born and it came time to give him a name, we chose Bob instead. He rarely visits; he never writes. Now, on occasion, I wish I'd named him Harry as well.

Strangely, I'm not bitter about what is happening to me. Why should I be? I am no better than anyone else. I am no wiser, no stronger, and no smarter. (Okay, I am smarter than ol' man Ross who lives next door but that's beside the point.) So then, why not me?

I hope to go quickly so I'll be remembered as Grandpa Harry and not as the person I'm becoming. I fear I'll be remembered as a contemptible, cranky old man and that thought sickens me. The fact is, I'm losing my mind. I have Alzheimer's—an insidious disease that causes the nerve cells in the brain to degenerate. As it works its havoc, the brain shrinks and wastes away—dementia sets in, causing disorientation and confusion. There is no cure, no way to slow its determined progression.

This disease is a thief. It begins with short spells of forgetfulness, but before it's finished, it steals everything. It takes your favorite color, the smell of your favorite food, the night of your first kiss, your love of golf. Droplets of shimmering water cleansing the earth during an invigorating spring shower simply become rain. Mammoth snowflakes blanketing the ground in white at the onset of winter's first storm merely seem cold. Your heart beats, your lungs suck in air, your eyes see images, but inside you are dead. Inside your spirit is gone. I say it is an insidious disease because in the end, it steals your existence—even your very soul. In the end I will forget Emily.

The disease is progressing, and even now people are beginning to laugh. I do not hate them for it; they laugh with good reason. I would laugh as well at the stupid things I do. Two days ago I peed in the driveway in my front yard. I had to go and at the time it seemed like a great spot. A week before, I woke up in the middle of the night, walked into the kitchen, and tried to gargle with the dishwashing liquid that is kept in the cupboard beneath the sink. I thought I was in the bathroom, and the green liquid was the same color as my mouthwash. I get nervous. I get scared, and I cry; I cry like a baby over the most ridiculous things. During my life, I've seldom cried.

There are times when I can still think clearly, but each day I feel my good time fading—my existence getting shorter. During my good spells, now just an hour or two a day, I sit at my desk and I write. I crouch over the keyboard on my computer and I punch the keys wildly. It's an older computer, but it serves its purpose well. It's the best gift Bob has given me in years. It's an amazing machine and every time I use it, I marvel at how it captures my words. Younger people who have grown up with computers around them don't appreciate the truly miraculous machines they are. They create magic.

I'm not a good writer, but I've loved writing stories and poems all of my life. Writing always made me feel immortal—as if I were creating an extension of my life that nothing could destroy. It was exhilarating.

I no longer write for excitement. There are times when

my back aches and my eyes blur, and I can't get my fingers to hit the right keys, but I continue. I write now for Emily. She is just seven years old. I doubt she'll remember my face; I doubt she'll remember the crooked fingers on my wrinkled hands or the age spots on my skin or my shiny, bald head. But hopefully, by some miracle, she will read my stories and my poems and she'll remember my heart, and consider me as her friend. That is my deepest desire.

At times I feel bad that I'm not writing to my other grandchildren, but I hardly know them. While they visit every Christmas, they don't stay long. They are courteous, but they treat me like a stranger. It's not their fault. I'm not angry with them, and I hope they aren't angry with me.

My worst fear is that before I finish, I will slip completely into the grasp of the terrible monster, never to return. If this happens, my prayer would be that those around me might forget—but they will not forget—and then, worse than being forgotten, I will be remembered as a different person than I truly am. I will be despised.

I vow not to let this happen, so during my good times, I write—I write for Emily.

CHAPTER *Two*

$\mathcal{I}$F YOU'LL NOTICE THE KITCHEN, MRS. HENDRICKS, THERE'S A sink in the corner below the window, as well as one on the center island. With two sinks and the double oven, this place would be fabulous for entertaining friends." She was trying not to rush the woman, but she'd been with her all morning, and both time and patience were running short. Emily would never let her hear the end of it if she showed up late again.

"I do like this place a lot, Laura. I just don't know," responded the plump, finicky woman. "Can we run back to the one on Pierpont and compare it, one last time?" It was posed as a question, but came out more like a command. Laura took a deep breath and tried not to let her frustration show.

"Absolutely, but I'd like to do it first thing tomorrow morning. I need to pick up my daughter from school in a few minutes, and she'll skewer me if I get there late."

"Tomorrow? Oh no, that won't do. I have my hair appointment in the morning, and I promised Charlie I'd decide between the two today." Laura detested such clients, but forcing a smile, she reminded herself how much she wanted this commission. While her initial reaction was to tell the woman to take a flying leap off the back deck, she continued calmly. "I'll tell you what, Mrs. Hendricks. Come with me to pick up Emily, my daughter, and after I drop her off to visit her grandpa, we'll run back up to the other house. Will that work?"

"Hmm, could you drop me off at the Pierpont house first? I'll just stay there and wander a bit until you can swing back and pick me up after your little errand."

It was not an errand, it was her daughter, and Laura was close to reaching her breaking point. "Certainly," she blurted as she headed to the front door. Right now, dumping "Cruella" anywhere seemed like a great option.

As she reached the school, she could see Emily standing on the curb. While she normally rode the bus, today was Friday. That meant Laura would pick her up and they'd head straight to Grandpa Whitney's house to visit.

"Mom! Hurry, we're gonna miss his good time."

"We'll be fine, honey. I'm so sorry. At least it's only fifteen minutes this time. Last time it was twice that. I'm making progress."

Emily didn't smile as she jumped into the car. "Okay, go!"

"So, how was school today?" Laura questioned, hoping to change the subject.

"It was good, 'cept for I colored my leaves purple and

Billy Mason said it was stupid to color leaves purple and then he took the purple crayon so I couldn't color and so I told teacher and Billy got in trouble." She hardly took a breath.

"Is that so? Well, what color did Billy use on his leaves?"

"He didn't have leaves. He drew a picture of a tank, but he colored it red and tanks aren't red, and it was stupid, but I didn't tell him."

"That was very kind of you, sweetie. Can I see your picture?"

"I didn't brung it home yet."

"Bring it," Laura corrected.

"But I'll show you my other papers." Anxiously unzipping her Old Navy backpack, she pulled out her notebook and gathered her papers.

As Laura watched the sun reflect off her daughter's shoulder-length brown hair, she could almost remember being seven herself. It was such an innocent age—full of adventure and learning.

Emily held out several papers for Laura to see. She swerved twice in traffic trying to look at them. "Honey, you'd better show me the rest when we get to Grandpa's house. I don't want to crash."

"Okay, Mom," she replied, stashing them back into the bag. "Are we there yet?"

"Just about."

"Mom?"

"Yes, dear."

"How come pigs don't wear clothes?"

Laura laughed. "What?"

"We wear people clothes, how come pigs don't wear pig clothes?"

Emily was always full of questions. Sometimes they were profound, sometimes bizarre, and often they were humorous.

"Next time you meet a pig, why don't you stop and ask him?"

Emily giggled. "Pigs don't talk, duh."

"You're right, honey. Pigs don't talk."

Several minutes passed as Emily appeared deep in thought.

"Mom?" she asked again, "Why don't pigs talk?"

"I'm not sure. Let's ask the cows," Laura joked.

Before Emily could respond Laura turned the corner in front of Harry's house. "Look, we're at Grandpa's now. Let's figure out the pigs later, okay?"

Harry's small brick house was located on Lincoln Street in Midvalley, a fifteen-minute drive from Emily's school in Lake Park. All of the homes in this section of town were well kept. Both sides of the street were lined with old-fashioned lamps which not only kept the area well lit, but also gave a nostalgic feeling to the neighborhood.

Harry had lived in the house most of his adult life. He'd built it with his own hands in the mid 1940s with help from his brother, a carpenter. It was his first house, and though later in life he could have afforded more, he could never bring himself to move. Perhaps it reminded him of life with Kathryn.

As Laura and Emily approached, they could see Cara's car parked in front at the curb.

"Oh good, Cara's here," Emily shouted. "I like her, she's funny."

Cara's business card read "*Independent In-Home Assistant to the Elderly.*" Though she was just twenty-six, her heavy build and full round features made her look ten years older.

Her dark black skin was a stark contrast to the bright white uniform she always wore. She might have been mistaken for a nurse; the truth was that she had dropped out of nursing school in Atlanta five years earlier after only one semester because she'd found it difficult to scrape the tuition money together. She'd begun in-home assistance after moving to the area four years ago to help take care of her aunt. She'd told Laura that while she wasn't getting rich, there always seemed to be plenty of customers, and the satisfaction she received from helping elderly people in need was exactly the reward she had sought when she chose nursing as a career.

Laura's husband, Bob, had hired Cara three months earlier when Harry's condition began to worsen. Initially she dropped in for a few minutes each morning, fixed breakfast, checked his condition and took care of any small needs. Lately, she had been spending a good part of her day at the house.

After the car came to a stop, Emily jumped out and ran up the steps to the front door. Without ringing the doorbell, she burst into the house and began searching for Grandpa Whitney and Cara.

"Hello? Hey, where is everyone?" she called out.

"Emily? That you?" Cara answered from the kitchen.

Emily bounded toward the sound of the voice. "Hi, Cara, how's Grandpa doing?"

Cara stood at the sink washing dishes but put down the wet plate to welcome the child with a high five. "Well, girl, I think he'd love a visit."

"Is he out back?"

"Sure enough. He's out on the porch," she replied, pointing toward the back door. Emily was gone in a flash. Laura caught just a glimpse of her blue pants streaking out the door.

"Hi there, Cara," Laura greeted.

"Hey, Laura. How y'all doin' today?"

"We're doing great. Late as usual, but still great."

"Is that a new 'do?" Cara asked.

"My hair?" Laura chuckled. "Yeah. I was getting tired of pulling out the gray. I had a weave last week. They lightened the brown a touch, but you're the first to notice."

"Really? Looks dynamite."

"Thanks. So, is he on the porch?"

"Yep, Emily's already there."

"Hang on, I'll be right back." Laura walked softly to the back door to eavesdrop on Emily's conversation. The old man sat in a reclining lawn chair under an aluminum-covered porch attached to the house. It was a pleasant place for Harry to sit and admire his garden.

"Hi, Grandpa," Emily greeted. There was no response from Harry. "I said hi, Grandpa," she repeated louder.

"Hell's bells, you don't have to yell."

"Grandpa, don't talk that way, it's not nice!"

"What's your name, anyway?" he asked, in a softer tone.

"Grandpa! You know my name. It's Emily."

"What a nice name, Amy."

"Grandpa, it's Emily, not Amy." She giggled. "So you want to play checkers again?"

He appeared confused at the question. She ignored his puzzlement and skipped over to the cabinet next to the back door to retrieve the game.

"You want black or red?"

"What?"

"I said do you want to be black or red?" No reply came. He watched intently as the little girl placed the colored plastic disks neatly on the checkered board. As Emily made the first move, his eyes brightened. He reached out with his bent finger and pushed the black plastic circle one spot forward.

"Listen, Emily," Laura called through the screen door, "I have to run a quick errand. You stay and visit with Grandpa for a while. I'll be back in thirty minutes. Cara's in the kitchen if you need anything."

"Okay, bye, Mommy. Your move, Grandpa." Laura watched the two for another moment, intrigued that a girl as young as Emily would have so much empathy for a crotchety old man. Smiling, she tiptoed back to the kitchen, so as not to disturb the game in progress.

"How's he really doing, Cara?"

"He's not doin' too good, Laura." She talked while she dried the last of the dishes. "He typed like a maniac in the mornin' for about ten minutes, but then he locked himself in the bathroom for almost an hour before he could figure out how to undo the lock. I almost called 911, but he wasn't screamin' and I figured he couldn't get into no trouble in there. It's just my opinion, but you may wanna start thinkin' 'bout getting him into a home. I hate to say it, 'cause I'd lose my best client, but I'd hate it worse to see Mr. Harry hurt himself or somethin'." It was the answer Laura dreaded but had been expecting. Harry had seemed despondent lately. She had sensed it was time for a change.

"Thanks, Cara. Sorry for the trouble. I'll call Bob tomorrow and talk over the timing with him. We'll figure out what to do this week. Is it okay if I let you know by next Friday?"

"Oh sure. And like I say, I don't mind being here, just give me a few days' notice once y'all decide."

"Thanks again. So, did Bob send you a check for last month?"

"I got it right on time, no problem. So how you two doin' anyway?"

Laura would often chat with Cara during the Friday visits, while Emily entertained Harry. Though they had become good friends, Laura still felt uncomfortable talking about her imminent separation from Bob.

"He's doing well. He seems to love his new job."

"I don't care how he's doin', how are you doin'?"

She hated getting emotional. It made her feel weak and dependent. Biting her lip, she vowed this time to be strong.

"I'm doing fine. We're still trying to work things out, but it doesn't look like we will." Her voice faltered slightly, but Cara didn't seem to notice.

"Men!" Cara pronounced with disgust. "They're the only reason I don't get married." Both started to laugh.

"Cara, I almost forgot, I have to run back up to the city. I left a client alone at a house, something I'm never supposed to do. Is it okay if Emily stays—are you going to be here a bit longer?"

"I'll be here, so don't you be worrying 'bout her."

"Thanks so much. I have my phone if there's a problem."

"Take whatever time you need."

Laura gave her a quick hug, then trotted to her car. After making sure her phone was on, she placed it on the passenger seat beside her and headed toward the house on Pierpont to pick up Mrs. Hendricks.

People were beginning to ask about Bob. What was she supposed to tell them when they asked how things were going? She had vowed not to get emotional when they asked, and she had done well in front of Cara. Yet now as she pulled away from the house, she wished she had told her friend the truth. She wished she had explained that makeup was covering dark circles under her eyes; that eye drops were helping to hide the red; that there were periods of such terrible heartache that a physical pain developed in her chest; that often she couldn't get to sleep in the evening or get out of bed in the morning; and during all of these times she worried about Emily. She knew people were whispering, wondering. What exactly was she supposed to say?

Six blocks away from the house she started to cry.

CHAPTER *Three*

*A*FTER A GLASS OF MILK, THREE COOKIES, AND TWO BEDTIME stories, Emily was tucked securely in bed with her two blankets pulled up tight against her chin.

The two-blanket ritual was one she had insisted on since the age of four. It had come about strictly by accident. When Emily's blanket was in absolute shreds, Laura had decided it was time for a change. It had been such a problem to get the ragged thing away from the child, even to wash, that the obvious answer seemed to be two new ones that could be alternated in washing. At least it seemed like the easy answer. When presented with the new blankets, Emily was sure she'd struck gold, ecstatic that she had twice as much as she had given up. The first night she placed a blanket on each side of her face, her mouth and nose barely peeking through. "Look at me. I'm a Eskimo," she exclaimed. Each night afterwards she insisted on sleeping with both blankets. The original problem had multiplied; now Laura had two blankets to wash.

"Are you all comfy and cozy?" Laura quizzed, kissing her on the cheek.

"Yep. Will you lay down with me?"

"I already read you two books. Just give me a hug, I have something I need to do in my room."

"Okay, night, Mom."

"Good-night, babe."

Laura clicked off the light and headed to the master bedroom. She glared at the stack of mail still sitting on the bed. Her queasiness returned. She had noticed the letter when sorting through the mail after they'd returned home from Harry's. In the usual mix of bills and bulk-rate junk mail was the crisp white envelope with the disturbing return address. She didn't want to cry in front of Emily, so she quickly mixed it back into the stack and tried to put it out of her mind. Now, in the quiet of her bedroom, she pulled out the envelope and stared—Bagley, Morris, and Lattimer, Attorneys at Law.

She had known it was coming. She and Bob had discussed it a few days ago, but at the time it hadn't seemed real. She'd clung to a glimmer of hope that the situation would work itself out. Now she sliced the envelope open with a fingernail file and removed the starched paper. It was addressed to her attorney with her name highlighted at the bottom under a section showing where copies had been sent. It read like a form letter with names plopped into place. But the letter she now held in her hands wasn't sent to "other people." It hadn't gone to a stranger, it was sent to her—and it meant that her marriage of eleven

years was crumbling before her eyes. It couldn't be happening, but in her hand she held the evidence—the beginning of the end.

It was a simple request to schedule a meeting with both
parties' attorneys so details of an amicable divorce settlement could be reached. But as she read, her eyes moist-
ened. What is it about me that he's grown to despise, she
wondered? Certainly they had had their share of arguments, but there had been good times as well, times of
laughter and fun when she felt so full of hope. Just weeks
before he had moved out, for example, they found themselves alone together in the middle of the day. They had
chased each other around the attic, both giggling like
schoolchildren. When he caught her, he pulled her to the
old couch in the corner, where they made love. It was sweet
and wonderful and she had wondered if it would be the
turning point to better times. Within days, however, they
were at odds again, arguing over the most trivial things.
And then three weeks later, his things were packed. He had
received the job offer and he was leaving for San Diego,
acting like it was no big deal—as if husbands abandoned
their families every day.

They had attempted counseling a year earlier, but after two
sessions, Bob refused to continue. She thought the sessions
went well; he felt like all the blame was being placed on him.
Had they grown apart? If so, then what about the good times,
she wondered? The thought of another woman entered her
mind again. If he was hiding someone, he was doing a great
job of it. She could find no evidence, and when she questioned Bob, he flatly denied that there was anyone else.

Laura dropped the letter onto the bed and hurried to the
bathroom to grab a tissue. She paused in front of the mirror

and studied her face. Slight wrinkles showed at the corners of her eyes. She had tried to cover them with makeup, but they still showed through. Could he be looking for someone younger? Had she married someone that shallow?

She returned to the bedroom with tissues in hand and curled up on the bed to consider her options. At eleven o'clock, when her tears had finally dried, she slipped out of her clothes and headed to the bathroom to take a shower. The water was warm and comforting, and she stayed in until the hot water ran out. She dressed for bed slowly, detesting the thought of sleeping alone again. The sheets were cold when she climbed in, and she shivered under the covers as she waited for the bed to warm. Forty-five minutes later, still awake, she rolled over and reached for the phone on the nightstand.

On the sixth ring he picked it up. "Hello?" He sounded dazed and in a strange way it gave her pleasure to have woken him up.

"Bob. It's me. Are you alone?"

"Laura, what's wrong? Is Emily okay?"

"She's fine, Bob, but I'm not okay." Her sorrow was turning to anger and she struggled to keep it under control.

"What? What's the matter, Laura?" he questioned, still trying to clear his head.

"So, is it really over, Bob? Just like that?" There was a noticeable pause before he responded.

"The letter—you got the letter, didn't you?"

"Of course I got the letter." She had wanted so badly to remain calm, but the anger inside was overpowering. "Did you think I'd call with excitement?"

"Laura, we talked about it. You knew it was coming."

"I knew it was coming? That's the point. After eleven

years of marriage, I didn't see it coming. I must be so stupid." She was starting to rant, and it was making him tense.

"Listen, just settle down. I'm talking about the letter. You knew it was being sent out. We talked about it. It's just a formality. It's the way attorneys do things. I'm coming out to see Emily next weekend. Let's talk then." He waited for her response and was surprised when none came.

"Laura? You there?"

"I'm here." She could feel grief again replacing her anger. "I'm here, Bob—I'm here, you're there, and there's going to be a little girl caught in between."

"Laura, just go to bed and get some rest. We'll talk about it some more next weekend. Okay? Oh, how's Dad doing? Is he all right?"

She paused. "He's fine, Bob, just fine." Clicking the phone back onto the stand, she rolled over and pulled the pillow over her head.

It was still dark outside when the alarm began to buzz. She wanted desperately to shut out the world and stay in bed. It had been a restless night with no sound sleep until the early hours of the morning. She smacked the snooze bar with her hand for ten more minutes of peace. In what felt like mere seconds, the alarm again ruined her dream. "Okay, okay," she yelled to the clock as it buzzed loudly, "shut up already!" When she checked Emily, she found her so sound asleep she decided to shower before waking her to get ready for school. If they were late, she'd drop Emily off on her way to the office. Ten minutes later she marched into Emily's room and turned on the light.

"Get up, sleepyhead. I let you sleep in, so you'll have to hurry to make the bus." Emily barely stirred. "Honey, get up so you won't be late for school." She moved to the bed and began to shake the sleeping child. With a slight moan, Emily turned over, looked at the clock, then sat up, rubbing her eyes. She looked puzzled.

"Hurry babe, get out of bed and get going." After a few pensive seconds, Emily looked at her mother and muttered, "Mommy, go back to bed, it's Saturday." With that she plopped backwards into the warmth of her blankets, still staring up at her mother's face.

The words caught Laura completely by surprise. She was bewildered as she paused to calculate the days. After a few seconds, they both began to laugh hysterically.

CHAPTER *Four*

A LIGHT RAIN WAS COMING DOWN AS BOB LACED ON HIS running shoes. Very few people other than joggers would be out this early. He was surprised at how easy it had been to get up this morning, having had so little sleep the night before. Why was Laura always so frenzied, especially in the middle of the night? Why couldn't she flip out at noon, or at dinnertime? Why always at midnight or one in the morning? He stepped into the garage, tied his key onto his shoe, and began to stretch. He'd started to run recently, after giving up tennis. It was a much better workout, and besides, the country club routine had become boring. Running on the beach at sunrise—now that was exercise.

When he felt he had stretched his legs enough, he stepped outside and headed in a slow trot toward the water. The beach was five blocks from his house, the perfect distance for warming up. The rain was more of a mist and would feel great in a few minutes.

The usual early morning joggers were making their way up and down the shore when he arrived, some on the trail, some on the sand. There were people he recognized who occasionally said "hello," but never anything more. They came to exercise, not to socialize. His muscles tightened as his shoes hit the dense, wet sand. He turned right. The routine was the same, a mile north to the pier and back, and then two miles in the opposite direction to the point. The round trip was just over six miles, plus the five blocks home, which he walked to cool down. He had been faithful, never missing a morning since he'd begun running, and it showed. Not only was he tan, but his muscles were also toned and solid; better than most thirty-six-year-old guys, he boasted to himself.

Though it was a weekend, he'd arranged to meet a group of young interns from the medical school for lunch. Get 'em while they're still young, the company always taught. He'd need a little time to prepare, but even so he'd still have a couple of hours to himself this morning. He wondered why he hadn't discovered running on the beach sooner. The sound of the water was soothing, and the morning salt air refreshing. He'd have to invite Emily out. She'd love the beach. He wondered if Laura would let her come. Did she have a choice? They couldn't seem to agree on anything lately, why would this be any different? Their relationship had grown to be so stifling. It was hard to pinpoint exactly when they'd become so distant from each other. He supposed it had been a slow process, occurring over several years. He knew Laura still held hopes that things would work out, but "work out" to Laura meant "Bob's fault." Take the marriage therapy sessions, for example.

"Tell me how you feel, Bob."

"I feel fine, thanks."

"No, tell me how you really feel."

Two more weeks of that and he thought he'd puke. If there was ever a disagreement, he was always to blame. "You're just not as sensitive as you used to be," she would say. He shook his head as he jogged. "What's that supposed to mean, anyway?" And Laura would get so worked up about the little things. The divorce letter, for example—she knew it was coming; they had talked about it last Friday, but still she calls in the middle of the night. It's not like I'm abandoning the family, he reasoned. He was willing to provide support for Emily. People get divorced all the time; what was the big deal? Laura had blamed his new job as the reason for their separation; couldn't she see it was just an excuse—an excuse to finally do something that had needed to be done for a long time? Yes, as far as he was concerned, the separation had been a success. A new place, a fresh start, life was going to be great. Laura would get over it. She was strong. She was more than strong—she was immutable. And Emily would understand when she was older.

His shirt was wet, partly from the morning mist, partly from sweat. As he reached the pier, he stripped it off and strapped it around his waist pack before heading back in the direction he'd come.

The job had been a dream. He had started with the pharmaceutical company in Lake Park. Though the company was terrific, his territory had been only mediocre; it was a rural area and there were only so many doctors to visit. Thank goodness they'd recognized his potential. Now his area covered a good chunk of Southern California, including San Diego, and his income had more than doubled. Other than the problems with his marriage, life couldn't be better.

"Bob? Bob Whitney?" He turned around at the sound of his name; a shapely young woman was calling to him. She looked familiar but he couldn't place her.

"It's Cynthia—Cynthia Jones, from Dr. Brightman's office," she added, as he stared blankly at her. Of course! She looked so different.

"Hi, how are you? I didn't recognize you without your nurse's uniform." She was wearing black jogging shorts and a white, oversized T-shirt; a black sports bra showed underneath it.

"Do you live around here?" she inquired.

"Yeah, actually I live on Westridge Road, about five blocks away."

"Oh, sure. I'm on Canterbury. I drive down and park in the lot while I run." Bob tried to think where Canterbury would be, but he was terrible at remembering street names.

"Do you jog here often?" he asked.

"Every morning, same time."

"I'm surprised I haven't seen you before."

"It is a big beach," she replied. "We've probably jogged right past each other and didn't pay attention."

He doubted that was possible, but nodded his head in agreement. A moment of odd silence followed, neither knowing what to say next.

"Well," she finally continued, "I better let you get back to your exercise." Then she added, "Maybe we could run together sometime?"

"Hey, that'd be great. I'll watch for you. And tell Mike that

I'll be in the office to see him later this week. I've got more samples to drop off."

"Sure thing. Take it easy now." She smiled, turned, and jogged away. As she headed down the beach, he admired her long tan legs, still amazed at how different she looked in jogging shorts.

Turning toward the point, he continued to run. Run together? Was she just being friendly or was she interested? He hadn't started dating yet. Not that he wouldn't have, had the opportunity come up. He'd been working extra hours getting the territory established, and that coupled with the biweekly trips to see Emily hadn't left much time to socialize. It would come with time. He turned back to see if he could still see her walking away, but she had gone. Picking up his pace, he sprinted beside the ocean waves rolling onto the sand. The salty mist was especially refreshing this morning. Running on the beach in the morning instead of playing tennis had been a terrific idea.

It was still dark when he opened his eyes and focused on the clock. Was it six in the morning, or was it the evening? He couldn't remember sleeping but was sure he had. It must be morning or it would still be light outside, he decided. Climbing out of bed, he dressed in his baggy brown trousers. He pulled his belt tight, causing his pants to ride high. Kathryn would be angry if he wore the same shirt he'd worn yesterday. Rummaging through the closet, he found one he hadn't remembered wearing in a few days and buttoned it up the front. It was hard to tie his shoes, so instead, he slipped on his brown house slippers and tiptoed to the kitchen. He didn't want to wake her. He had always been a morning person, but she liked to sleep late. Besides, Kathryn was in a better mood the rest of the day when he let her get her rest.

In the kitchen he took out six Saltine crackers and spread them thick with butter. There was still buttermilk in the refrigerator so he poured himself a glass. He ate standing. He still had a lot to do, and if he sat too comfortably at the table, he might not get up.

The shed was dark inside when he opened the door. He waved his hand wildly in the air searching for the string, and as it snagged on the flannel of his shirt, the light clicked on. The workbench was just as he'd left it yesterday—or the day before. If only he could finish the cover today, he still might make it in time. He surveyed what needed to be done and with a glimmer in his eye, he opened the lower drawer and removed the false bottom. If they only knew. He giggled like a child. The twinkle of gold in the drawer caused him to pause and reflect. Kathryn had loved the color gold. She looked like a queen when she tried on her gold dress. He could feel his mind slipping and forced himself to focus— he needed to finish or they might never know.

He worked slowly but methodically. It was not a difficult task, but it would take some time to get it perfect. If only his fingers worked the way they used to—before the disease had infected his body.

He pulled the fabric over the cover and held it in place, waiting for the glue to set. With his hands still, his mind drifted.

When she woke, they would pack their camping gear into the old Ford and then head to the mountains for the week-end. The wildflowers would be in bloom and the weather pleasant. They could pitch their tent by the stream in their usual spot and then drift to sleep in each other's arms to the sound of babbling water. He would rise early and cook bacon and eggs over the fire as the sun's early rays drifted over the trees and through the tent door. When she opened her eyes, she would find breakfast ready, and they would eat and then run after each other through the meadow, like they had done so many times before. If the day was hot enough, and if she was in the right mood, perhaps they would even swim naked again in the stream, and he would kiss her and tell her again that he was sorry and she would whisper to him that it was okay, that she still loved him.

The sound of the car startled him. How long had he been standing, holding the fabric? It was firm, the glue set. He would have to stop for today with only one complete. The others would have to wait until tomorrow; he would concentrate better tomorrow. Sliding the drawer closed, he pulled the string on the light and shuffled to the back porch. He was tired and needed to sit and rest.

Cara found him perched peacefully in his favorite chair.

"Mornin', Harry. You're up early." He didn't speak.

"What would you like for breakfast this morning?" She didn't expect him to answer. He seldom did. He would usually eat whatever she fixed, so today it would be either oatmeal or grits.

As she headed back to the kitchen, he turned his head toward her.

"Today, I'd like bacon and eggs. Bacon and eggs, and then I'm going to swim naked in the stream."

CHAPTER *Five*

LAURA WORRIED ABOUT THE LETTER. SHE'D NEVER received a letter from an attorney before and it bothered her—so intrusive and demanding. She called her attorney first thing Monday morning to get some advice. He assured her it was strictly routine. With attorneys' busy schedules and with Bob in town only every other weekend, he guessed it would be at least four weeks before a meeting could be set up. "A lot can happen in four weeks," he said. "Just be patient and try not to get emotional." She knew that he was right but the ease with which he delivered the advice made him seem cold and unfeeling. Couldn't he see that eleven years of her life were being crushed? She was sure he was either single or that the divorce business had turned him callously cold. Rather than argue, Laura agreed to take his advice. She would wait to see what Bob had to say this weekend.

Work at the office had been hectic, for which she was thankful. The busy schedule had helped keep her mind off the situation. By her boss Grant Midgley's account, Laura was terrific, especially for someone so new to the business. She had taken the position as a sales agent two months earlier, after graduating from real estate school and passing the state exam with flying colors. The decision to pursue a career came shortly after Bob had moved to San Diego. Though she didn't need the money, as he continued to provide for her and Emily, the uncertainty of the future pushed her forward.

Real estate had seemed like a natural. Her father had been an agent his entire life. Industry buzzwords were already familiar to her, so the rest came easily. She was articulate, bright, and when not discussing the breakup of her marriage, possessed a good sense of humor. She dressed professionally and looked the part of a skilled sales agent. It was a job she enjoyed, but also one in which she could juggle her time to accommodate Emily.

Midgley Real Estate had just been hired to represent the new River Meadows development near the mountains, and since the newspaper ads had run on Sunday, the phone hadn't stopped ringing. Tuesday had been Laura's turn to stay late at the office and answer calls, so she had arranged for Emily to play at their neighbors' house next door. Wednesday and Thursday were spent parading people through the model home. Several prospects looked promising. The best news of the week came Friday morning, when Mrs. Hendricks called to announce she had decided on the

Pierpont house. An offer was prepared, signed, and accepted. The home was huge, and the commission would be substantial. Laura left the office early to meet Emily and celebrate. She arrived at the school before class had been let out.

"Come on, babe," she teased, as Emily approached. "I can't wait for you all day."

"Mom, you're early?" She seemed shocked.

"Of course, it's the new me."

"Oh, I see." Her sarcasm sounded so grown-up that it made Laura smile.

"I have good news."

"Is Daddy coming today?"

"Well, yes, he comes tonight, but that's not the good news. I sold the big house to the older lady I told you about."

"The mean lady?" she questioned. Laura winced, not remembering how she'd described her.

"She was mean, but I like her now."

"Are we gonna pick Dad up tonight?" Emily asked, not at all interested in Laura's success.

"No, honey, he usually just gets a car at the airport." The first few weeks, Laura had picked up Bob for each visit home. As tension grew, he stopped asking and she stopped offering.

"Mom, how much longer is Daddy going to have to work in San Diego?" Her questions made Laura uncomfortable. They had never explained to her the extent of their problems. Laura didn't want to traumatize her needlessly if things could be worked out. It was the job that kept Dad away, they always told her. Laura wondered now if she'd repeated the lie for her own sake rather than for Emily's.

"I'm not sure, honey. His job is working out pretty well."

"How come we don't move there then?"

"So many questions today."

"Well?"

Bob had asked Laura to come with him when he accepted the job, but their arguments had reached a peak, and at the time it seemed to her that he wanted an excuse to move away. Ultimately, they decided the separation would be a test, a test that would reveal whether there was anything to salvage from their marriage.

"He wants to make sure the job works out first." She knew it was a lie. She knew Emily sensed things were not right.

"Are you and Dad getting divorced?"

"What do you know about divorce?" Laura quizzed, avoiding Emily's question.

"Well, Jenny's parents got divorced and now Jenny says they hate each other. Do you hate Dad?"

"Of course not, babe, we just have some problems we're trying to work out. We've grown apart." It was trite, but the best she could do.

"What does that mean anyways?" she persisted.

"It means that we don't get along anymore."

Emily sat quiet for a moment. "My teacher says if we don't get along, we have to sit next to each other during recess 'till we become friends again."

"Now there's a thought," Laura whispered. "Hey, I was thinking we could go for ice cream before Grandpa's to celebrate my selling the big house. You want to do that?"

"Nah, I hate ice cream."

"Since when? Banana-nut sundaes with caramel sauce are your favorite."

"Not no more."

Laura didn't bother correcting her. "Okay, babe. No problem." But Laura knew there was a problem, a big problem. She had watched families divorce before, and it was always the kids who were left with the most scars. She wasn't going to let that happen to Emily.

She pulled up to the curb in front of Harry's house and shut off the engine. Emily burst from the car and ran toward the door. By the time Laura entered the kitchen, Emily was already in the backyard.

"Hi again, Cara," Laura greeted.

"Hey, Laura. Is Emily okay? She hardly noticed me. Ran straight out back like her pants were on fire."

"I think she is catching on that bad times are coming. It scares her—it scares me, actually."

"I'm sorry. Guess it's gettin' worse with Bob?"

"You could say that. I got my first attorney letter this week. So it starts . . ."

"Listen, honey, you just hang in there. You got a good attorney, don't you?"

"I guess. They all seem the same to me—so heartless. I just don't want to be bitter. I don't want Emily to be hurt."

"Nobody does, but trust me when I tell you to get a mean attorney. You'll be thankin' me later."

Knowing she meant well, Laura looked her in the eye and spoke softly. "Cara, thanks for your friendship. Really, it means so much."

"Don't say it, woman, don't say it. You'd be my friend just the same if I were in your shoes."

"I know, but thanks. And I hate to ask," Laura said, changing the subject, "but how's Harry been this week?"

"Oh, Lordy, we had quite the time yesterday," she chuckled.

"What happened?"

"Oh, my, it was something."

"What? Are you just going to sit and laugh all day or tell me?"

"Okay, okay. Harry's real quiet for what must be almost a half-hour. That should have clued me in right there."

"Keep going," Laura prodded.

"Well, I thought we'd gathered up all the cans of gold spray paint, but I guess he must have had one hidden in the shed somewhere."

"Oh, no."

"Oh, yes. He's real quiet, so I finally go out to check on him, and you know the green lawn chair?"

"Yes."

"Well, it ain't green no more. It's now a gold lawn chair." Laura started to laugh as Cara continued. "And when I go out to find him, he was sittin' right in the middle of it—gold paint all over him, but smilin' like he was the king of the world. I didn't have the heart to scold him. Just let him sit there for over an hour. Had to peel him out of it by the time lunch was ready."

"You're a dear, Cara." Laura's voice then turned serious. "Is he coherent at all any more?"

"Not much. Did y'all have time to figure out what to do about gettin' him into a home?"

"I meant to, but we didn't get that far. I'm sorry. Bob's coming out tonight and I got all the crying out of me, so I promise it will be tonight for sure."

"Listen, honey, you got problems a lot more serious than Harry. You talk 'bout them first."

"Thanks, Cara. We will get it figured out one way or another." Just then Emily burst into the kitchen crying hysterically.

"What is it, Emily?" Laura asked, jumping to her feet.

"Grandpa spit on me," she blurted out through her tears.

"He what?" Laura could hardly believe her ears.

"See!" Emily held out her leg for both of them to see. Laura grabbed a tissue from her purse as Emily continued in a sob. "He was spitting on the floor. I told him to stop but he didn't. He kept doing it and then he spit on my leg. It was so gross. He yelled at me and then he knocked the checkers all over. I wanna go."

Cara headed out the back door. "I'll go have a talk with him."

"It's just so yucky," Emily whimpered. Laura held her tight, trying to calm her down.

"Let's go home. I wanna go home, and I don't wanna come here anymore."

"Emily?" Laura scolded lightly. "That doesn't sound like my girl."

"It's true."

Cara headed to the basement to retrieve a mop and didn't see Harry come in the back door. He stood in the hallway, behind the folding door that separated it from the kitchen where Emily clung to her mother.

"I never wanna come here again!" she repeated defiantly.

If the confused old man understood Emily's words, it didn't show in his face. His hands, clasped together, moved nervously back and forth in the air, his stare distant, as if the door and the walls were not there. His mind seemed to be in another time or place, unaware of his surroundings and the events that had just occurred. Yet, as Cara's footsteps sounded up the stairs and Harry shuffled toward the back door, a single tear rolled down his cheek.

CHAPTER Six

LAURA STOOD IN THE ARRIVALS TERMINAL WATCHING BOB move through the gate and walk past the crowd. Today he was wearing faded jeans and a navy T-shirt. A denim baseball cap covered his short dark hair. Some weekends he arrived in a suit and tie, running to the airport straight from an appointment; today he'd obviously had time to swing by his place first. He carried a black leather carry-on bag, and, noticing his tanned muscular arms, she guessed he'd been spending time at the gym. Without looking around, he headed down the terminal in her direction. He walked with confidence—the trait that had first attracted her to him so many years ago. When he passed within inches of her, she spoke his name.

"Hi, Bob." He jolted to a stop.

"Laura?" He seemed genuinely surprised to see her waiting. "What are you doing here? Is Emily here?"

"No, I left her with a babysitter. Bob, we need to talk." As soon as the words left her lips, she regretted her stupidity. It was the wrong thing to say.

"Whoa! I know I said we should talk when I got here, but you don't waste any time, do you?"

"I'm sorry. I didn't mean it to sound that way. It's not about us, Bob. We need to talk about Harry."

"Harry? Is he okay?"

"It's not a medical emergency or anything, but no, he's not okay. Let's get your bags and I'll explain in the car."

On the way home, Laura detailed the incident with Emily at Harry's that afternoon, in addition to others that had occurred in the past weeks. Bob listened intently.

"We need to get him into a home, Bob. I promised Cara we'd figure something out this weekend."

"A home, this weekend?"

"Yes, tomorrow."

"Can't the crazy old man wait another week? I have to fly out early in the afternoon on Sunday. I have a meeting with two regional vice presidents first thing Monday morning. This couldn't have come at a worse time."

"Sorry to inconvenience you, Bob, but it's your father we're talking about here."

"I know who it is. Don't lecture me." Not ten minutes from the airport and their discussion had evolved into an argument.

Laura had already figured out her plan. "Stop the car, Bob."

"What?"

"I said, stop the car. I won't do this. Let me out now if this is how we're going to continue."

He backed off. "Look, I'm sorry, I'm under a lot of pressure at work. I'm sorry." Laura took a deep breath and continued.

"I called several places this afternoon. Two of them actually have open houses tomorrow and I have appointments with two others. We can even take your dad if you think it's a good idea."

"Tomorrow," he repeated, more as an acceptance than a question.

"First thing. In fact, if it's okay with you, why don't you just sleep in the guest room again? That'll save us time in the morning. Do you think we should take Harry along or not?"

"No, let's narrow it down first."

"I agree."

"What does Emily think of all this?" Bob questioned.

"She was angry at him this afternoon, but she'll get over it. I'm not sure how she'll react to him moving into a rest home. It's just so sad to see him this way."

"Any way, for that matter," Bob muttered under his breath.

"What?" she questioned.

"Nothing. Nothing at all."

Emily could smell breakfast cooking and hurried down the stairs in her nightgown. As she turned the corner into the kitchen, Bob, wearing a large white apron, stood at the stove, flour dusting his cheek.

"Hi, darling. Ready for some pancakes?"

"Daddy!" She was thrilled to have him home and ran to give him a hug.

"How's my favorite daughter been doing this past week?" he asked, as he bent over to give her a squeeze.

"Duh, Daddy, I'm your only daughter."

"Duh?" he questioned, "Where'd you learn that?"

"I dunno," she replied, shrugging her little shoulders. "What are we gonna do today?"

He wasn't sure how to break the news. "Your mom will be down in a bit, and then we can all talk about it."

"Cool. Is Mom coming?"

"Sort of. As soon as she comes down, we'll discuss it—so what did you learn in school this week?"

"Nothin'. "

"What do you mean, nothin'? You must have learned something?"

"I drawed you a picture."

"You mean you drew me a picture."

"Duh, it's the same thing."

"Honey, you're a talkin' like thar ain't none difference n' I'ma tryin' ta tell ya that thar is." Bob was being silly, and Emily giggled as he continued. "Ware ya larnen to done talk tharta way, anyhows?"

"You have no idea," Laura piped in, entering the kitchen. "I thought I smelled something burning."

"Oh, no!" Bob turned back around to the stove and flipped the black pancake over. Then, in one quick motion, he tossed it into the sink across the counter. "That one was just to warm up the pan. That's the way we professional cooks do it." Laura rolled her eyes and walked over to the table.

"So, where we going today, Mommy?" Emily quizzed.

"Listen, babe," Laura knelt down as she spoke, "your dad and I need to run a few errands this morning. They're for Grandpa Whitney. Amie from next door is going to come over and play with you for two or three hours."

"Two or three hours!" she exclaimed. Laura knew it would probably take longer but hated to break it to her now.

"We'll hurry. It's just something important that we need

to do while your dad's here. Be good and we'll go to the park this afternoon. Okay?"

"Everybody?" Emily questioned. Laura looked up at Bob, not sure how to answer.

"Of course everybody," Bob chimed in. "We'll all have a picnic at the park together."

Understanding she had no choice, and with the promise of a picnic with both of her parents, Emily agreed. As Bob placed the first stack of good pancakes on Emily's plate, Laura headed upstairs to change.

The first stop on their list was the least expensive of the two that would quote prices over the phone. Bob turned into a parking space and shut off the car. There was a huge lawn in front, but the grass was long and matted, badly in need of care. The building was dingy brown with a sidewalk that was cracked and uneven leading up to the front door.

"You sure about this one?" Bob asked.

"It must be better inside," Laura insisted. "Come on, let's at least have a look."

She had expected dozens of friendly older couples, perhaps sitting around in groups of two or three, playing cards or watching TV, waving happily to any visitors. There were old people all right, but no cards were in sight. The lobby was littered with aging bodies, many in wheelchairs, others perched on stained furniture in crowded rows. Some stared silently at Bob and Laura, while others gazed into the distance. The odor was clinical.

"Is this the morgue?" Bob questioned, loud enough for others to hear.

"Bob, quiet!" Laura scolded as they walked toward a sign across the lobby that read "Welcome."

"This place should be on *Sixty Minutes*," he added.

"I said stop that," Laura insisted, turning to glare in his direction.

"Be careful," he warned, "you'll start to look like they do."

She stopped dead in her tracks and gazed around the room. She knew he was right. There were no smiling faces or welcoming glances, no friendly exchanges or affectionate waves—only vacant, lonely, pitiful stares.

"Bob, you're right. This is creepy. Let's get out of here."

"What? I was only kidding."

"No, you were right. Let's go now."

"I'm right? Will you put that down on paper and sign it?"

"Sure. Let's just go." Turning around, they picked up their pace to a trot as they headed back toward the door. In the safety of their car, Laura sighed deeply. "I guess we can cross that one off the list."

"I don't know," Bob replied, "Harry would have fit right in."

"Bob, don't say things like that. At least try to be civil."

Bob didn't say anything, knowing that if he continued he was bound to get the "if you can't say something nice, don't say anything at all" lecture.

The second stop went much better. The place was clean and more cheerful than the first. But it was the third home on their list, WestRidge Assisted Living Center, that impressed Laura.

An elderly woman who introduced herself as Mrs. Drucilla Haddley greeted them at the door. She informed them that it was her turn to be the Saturday greeter and that she had made the chocolate chip cookies. In a polite but firm tone, she assured them that her cookies were much better than those that had been purchased at the store.

The walls in the lobby were painted in up-to-date colors,

making the atmosphere almost seem cheery. After visiting with Mrs. Haddley and two of her friends who'd wandered over, Bob and Laura were introduced to Dr. Shanon Crosby, the head of the center. She appeared to be in her mid fifties, with dark hair pulled like a schoolgirl's into a ponytail. As they sat down in her office, they noticed a degree in geriatrics from Stanford hanging on the wall.

"It's so good to have you visit our facility today on behalf of Harry." Laura was impressed she had remembered his name, and from only one phone conversation. Dr. Crosby turned to address Bob. "Now, if I recall correctly from your wife's phone call, Harry is your father?"

"Yes, that's correct," he replied.

"Let me tell you both a little about our philosophy here at WestRidge. We're different than most." You can say that again, Laura thought, as the doctor continued. "Some people are strong and coherent until the day they die, but unfortunately, others aren't. We offer three specific levels of care, ranging from considerable independence to extensive assistance. We want to make sure older people enjoy the highest possible quality of life—in comfort and dignity."

"How do you know when someone is ready for a place like this?" Bob questioned.

"That's a hard question to answer, and it depends on the individual. You do need to understand, though, that it's difficult for any child to make the decision to admit a parent. By considering a center such as ours, you aren't abandoning Harry. If he could be a danger to himself, then you're actually getting him the help he needs. I had to put my mother in a home, years ago. That's partly why I chose to get involved in this part of the healthcare industry. I've tried to create a place where I'd like to stay when I get to that point in my life." She knocked on her wooden desk. "What other questions?"

Bob spoke again. "Harry, uh, Dad, is not, how shall I say it, he's not well all of the time. Can you handle . . ." He wasn't sure how to describe him.

She had heard this question many times and answered before he even finished his sentence. "We employ trained professionals, from doctors and nurses to elderly-patient-care-personnel. They handle the problems of old age every day and have been trained to know what to do. If you decide to admit Harry, I'll need to see his medical file. But barring a major medical problem that would require hospitalization, we can treat all the symptoms of aging right here."

Bob continued, "Do you have a fee schedule?"

"Yes, sir. Of course." Pulling a packet of information from a stack behind her desk, she handed it to him. "This will answer all of your questions, including your financial ones. Now, anything else, or are you ready to take the tour?"

Laura was ready to sign up right there, tour or no tour. Bob seemed in less of a hurry. "Sure, we'd like to see what you have to offer," he replied.

Stepping from her office into the lobby, Dr. Crosby introduced them to a young girl who looked to be of college age. She was wearing a white uniform. "This is Samantha Peterson, one of our staff. She will take you around and show you the facilities. We have three different types of rooms. Will Harry be doing his own cooking?" Bob and Laura looked at each other with surprise and then shook their heads in unison. "No! It would be best to not let him near the stove," Bob added.

"No problem at all. Samantha will show you all three

rooms anyway, so you can see the differences, plus she'll explain the various levels of service we offer. As I told you, some elderly people need very little help, others need extensive assistance. We accommodate both ends of the spectrum and anything in between. You're also welcome to have lunch with us in the dining room at noon. Afterwards, let me know what you think of our facility." She shook their hands again warmly and departed to meet her next appointment, a young woman and elderly man, waiting outside her office.

Samantha, though young, was professional and cordial. She had obviously given the tour many times. They started with the living quarters. The rooms appeared clean and well kept. Some had kitchens with two separate bedrooms, others just a single bedroom and bathroom. The dining room was impressive as well. Rather than long rows of rectangular tables strung together, there were round tables placed in groups, each with its own unique centerpiece.

Next came the recreation rooms, all painted bright solid colors, each one named according to the color of the paint. The "red" room was the largest, with two televisions at each end. Three couches on coasters lined one side, ready to be swung into the middle of the room for easy television viewing. Two other couches were positioned in front of a TV at the far end. Three elderly women and a man sat enthralled watching *Wheel of Fortune*. "This room's generally used for visiting and watching TV. We have video night on Mondays and Fridays. On Mondays the women choose what we watch, and we usually see love stories. On Fridays it's the men's turn, and they tend to select war movies."

Laura smiled at the thought.

"Next door we have two smaller rooms, 'green room one' and 'green room two.' I have no idea why we have two green rooms—leftover paint, I imagine. These rooms hold our card tables and chairs. We've got some people here who can play a mean game of gin rummy."

"No poker?" Bob questioned jokingly.

"Actually, they've been known to sneak in a hand of that as well. But don't play against Mrs. Wellington, trust me on that one. She used to be a dealer in Vegas—she'll have you sitting in your underwear in no time."

As they continued their stroll down the wide hall, the next room caused Laura's heart to jump.

"This is our puzzle room, and as you can see it's called the . . ."

"The gold room!" Laura finished. The room held six card tables, and stacks of jigsaw puzzles filled a shelf against the far wall. Two puzzles in progress covered two of the tables. Laura was ecstatic. "Can you believe it, Bob? They have a gold room!"

"He likes gold?" Samantha inquired.

"You have no idea," Laura replied. "He's going to sit in here and never come out."

If Bob was impressed, he tried not to let it show. He nodded and looked around, as if he spent every day touring similar establishments. After the gold room, they took a quick walk around the grounds outside before coming full circle back to the main lobby.

"Would you like to join us for lunch?" Samantha asked as they reached the front entry.

They looked at each other, trying to communicate silently. Bob spoke up.

"We appreciate it, but there are a couple of other places

we still need to see. Your facilities are very nice, though, and thank you so much for the impressive tour."

"No problem at all. I hope it's been to your liking—oh, here comes Dr. Crosby now."

Laura could hardly contain her excitement. "Dr. Crosby, it's absolutely wonderful. Bob and I need to discuss it, but we're impressed with everything you've done here. Again, absolutely wonderful."

"I'm glad to hear that. If you want to bring Harry back, we'd love to show him around as well. The open house runs until six tonight."

Laura almost danced to the car. "Bob, it's perfect. And they have a gold room." She shook her head in disbelief.

Bob rifled through the packet until he found the price sheet. He scanned it thoroughly. "Well, it should be nice, it's two and a half times the price of the first one and twice the last, and that's for the smallest room!"

"It should be more. You saw the place—it's not only nice, it's perfect. I think we should go get Harry right now and bring him to see it."

"Laura, I've been sending Cara a check faithfully, but it's starting to add up. This place is great, but it's expensive. Should we sell Dad's house to pay for it? He could live for ten more years."

Laura was disgusted that he showed so much concern for the money and so little regard for the welfare of his own father. Instead of having the conversation erode into another argument, she decided just to agree. "We probably should sell his house. After all, if he moves in here, nobody would be living there. It only makes sense. Let's give him a couple of months though, just to make sure everything works out."

He was taken aback by her response. "Just like that?"

"Bob, you saw the place."

What could he say now that she had concurred so readily? "Well, I guess we could go get Harry and show him around."

On the way back, Laura couldn't stop talking about their find. "It was everything I'd hoped for and more. And Dr. Crosby was incredible."

"You did good, Laura. Harry's going to love it," Bob conceded.

"I still don't understand why you insist on calling him Harry."

"That's his name. What am I supposed to call him?"

"What's wrong with 'Dad'? Our whole married life, you've used his first name. Was it just to irk him, 'cause you two didn't get along?"

The question seemed to catch Bob off guard. After several seconds, he answered, "I guess Harry just seemed to fit better than Dad." He winced as he said the word.

"Was he really that bad?" Over eleven years of marriage, he'd always brushed off discussions about his relationship with his father. At best it was cordial, but never close. The first few years she questioned him about the problem, but as he hated discussing it, she seldom pursued it.

To her surprise he continued, "I guess I never felt like he cared about us, Laura. He was always so distant. We could never seem to talk to him about anything."

"Was it always his fault?"

"Why are we psychoanalyzing my relationship with Harry now?" he asked.

"No big deal. I guess I was just curious." She was willing to drop it. He kept talking.

"If he'd been overly demanding, I think I could have handled it just fine. The problem, Laura, was he just didn't give a damn. He didn't care. I understand that he went through a lot with losing Mom so early. I realize it was traumatic for him, but he never seemed to understand that Michelle and I lost a mother as well. We had no mother, and yet we didn't give up on the family." His anger was apparent. "I got out as soon as I could. Anywhere was better than being around him."

"I shouldn't have brought it up. I'm sorry, Bob." He didn't reply.

When they arrived at Harry's, Cara's car was nowhere in sight. She'd been practically living there of late, so Laura was surprised to find Harry alone. He sat contentedly at the kitchen table.

Laura spoke first. "Harry, how are you?"

"Fine." He looked up, his gaze landing on Bob.

"Hi, Harry." Bob greeted.

"Bob? What are you doing here?" He was ornery, but at least coherent.

"I'm fine too, Harry," Bob responded, ignoring the question and his tone.

"I thought you moved to Sacramento?"

"It's San Diego, but at least you got the state right."

"Where's Emily?" Harry asked. Laura was surprised at how alert he was today.

"She's at home. We have something we want to show you."

"Do I have to get up?"

"Yes, we're going in the car." Bob moved to help him up, but Harry grabbed the table and stood by himself.

"'Bout time somebody took me somewhere." He shuffled across the room. "I have to go to the bathroom first."

"Take your time, Harry," Laura replied.

"He seems normal to me," Bob responded, once Harry had shut the door.

"This is the best I've seen him in weeks, Bob. It's so nice to see him doing well." Bob shrugged, not sure if the stories he'd been hearing had been exaggerated.

After Harry had retrieved his jacket from the bedroom, Bob helped him into the car. "Glad you two are back together again. Downright stupid to be apart in the first place." Laura smiled, but didn't say a word, happy the old man was on her side.

"We appreciate your help, but we can work out our own problems," Bob added.

During the drive they began to prepare him for the visit. "Seems to me that house is getting old," Bob began.

"I built it, you know. Did it myself. Didn't draw the plan, but I built the rest."

"I know, you've mentioned that before. Those basement stairs can be dangerous if you're not careful. It'd be awful if you slipped down them."

"Don't hardly go down 'em at all. That black woman, though, she might fall down 'em. You should talk to her. So, where's Emily?"

"We left her with a sitter, Harry. I'll bring her by next Friday," Laura replied. He didn't answer but seemed content with her response.

Bob continued. "We found a really nice place we want you to look at. There are lots of friendly people living there. We thought you might want to check it out, see if you'd like it better than your house."

"I built my house, you know, with my own hands. 'Course, Arty helped me. He's a carpenter, you know."

"Arty's been dead for decades now, Harry." Bob was getting impatient. Laura hadn't seen Harry this talkative in weeks.

"'Course he's dead. I know that. We use to hunt together on weekends, up Black Fork canyon. Yep, Arty the carpenter. Couldn't shoot worth a hill a beans, but he was good with a hammer. Helped me build it and all."

Reaching the center, they parked in a handicap stall near the entrance. Harry looked directly at the sign, reading "WestRidge Assisted Living Center" but didn't seem to register its meaning. Mrs. Haddley had been replaced at the front door by a new greeter—an older gentleman, much less talkative than Mrs. Haddley, but still pleasant.

"Do you want some punch and cookies, Harry?" Laura asked.

"Whose birthday is it?" he questioned.

"It's not a birthday party. We wanted to bring you down and show you around," she continued.

"What is this place anyway?"

"Isn't it great? We thought you'd like it much better here than at your old house." Her answer caught him off guard and he cocked his head toward her, not sure he'd understood.

"You want me to live here? Move out of my house?"

Bob answered next. "Exactly. It's getting hard to take care of you there, and we thought you'd like it better here. They even have a room painted completely gold. You'd have your very own apartment, all your own things."

Harry's countenance turned dark.

"What are you trying to do, steal my house? You're trying to steal my house!"

They were shocked by his reaction. "We don't care about your house, Harry," Bob replied. "We're just trying to take care of you, get you into a better situation."

"You never visit, and when you do, you try and take what's mine!"

"Harry, we aren't trying to take anything."

"You two-faced cheat, trying to steal the house I built with my own hands. You two-faced cheat!" He was raising his voice, causing the people in the lobby to stare.

"Harry, you're getting out of control here. We just thought you'd like this place better. They have people who can take good care of you here."

"I can take care of myself," he shouted. "I don't need help from you, you lying cheat!"

Hearing the commotion, Dr. Crosby came out of her office and headed in their direction to assist. She motioned to two assistants for help.

Laura spoke next, trying to calm him down. "Harry, we just want what's best for you, honestly. We thought you'd like it here, but if you don't, that's fine. You don't have to stay."

At this point, he wasn't listening or he didn't understand. "You all want me dead. You want me to die here, so you can take my house." He turned to face Bob. "You're just a good for nothing son!"

"Harry, my name is Dr. Shanon Crosby," she interrupted. "I run the center. I understand how you feel."

"I'm getting outta here, before you all try to kill me!" He was about to run when Bob reached out and grabbed on to his pants to keep him from leaving. As he did, Harry turned toward him trying to swing his fists. "I'll kill you, you dirty crook, you dirty lying crook." The two assistants, who had come to help, reached out to restrain him. They seemed unfazed by the outburst and helped carry Harry over to a chair where they forced him to sit. As they did, he began to struggle wildly, crying in a high-pitched voice.

"Kathryn, they're killing me! Put me down! Thieves!" They held on to him firmly as he continued to squirm.

Laura started to cry. Dr. Crosby reached out and took her by the hand.

"Come with me, Laura, and sit in my office. He'll be just fine. Honestly, we see this all the time."

After a few minutes, Harry's struggle subsided. The men holding him let go as he relaxed into a trance.

Bob walked over to his father's side. "Are you okay?" he asked. Harry refused to answer.

Dr. Crosby waved Bob into her office while one of the aides continued to sit by Harry's side. She motioned for Bob and Laura to sit, closed the door, and took a seat beside them. "If it's any consolation, you've been through the worst part. I know it's hard to believe, but he will thank you later. Many of our patients reacted in similar ways. If you ask them now, they just laugh about it."

"We were only trying to help him," Laura answered through her tears. "We didn't mean to upset him."

"It's one of the hardest things a child will have to do. You feel guilty, you feel like you're betraying your parents, like you're turning your back on them, passing off your responsibility to take care of them. I don't have all the answers for you. Every situation is different. But in most cases, it's the best thing for them. No matter how much you love them, there comes a point when everyone needs help. We children often have good intentions, but the reality is that we can't offer the elderly the care they sometimes need."

Laura seemed relieved at the words. Bob spoke next. "So, what papers do we need to fill out?"

"Everything needed for admitting Harry is in your packet. We do all intakes on Thursdays. I'm sorry, but we can't do any more until next Thursday. We could schedule him then, if that's what you want to do."

"That will be just fine. We'll have him ready."

When they arrived back at the house, Cara was parked out front and she was frantic. When she noticed Harry in the car with Bob and Laura, she sighed deeply.

"Am I glad to see you! I thought he'd run off. I've been drivin' around lookin' for him. I was just about to call and tell you he was missin.'"

Laura touched her shoulder. "We're so sorry. We completely forgot to leave a note. You weren't here when we arrived, so it just slipped our minds." Harry sat in the car, still distant and aloof.

"No problem, I'm just glad to see he's not runnin' naked in the street somewhere."

Bob opened Harry's door and helped him out.

Cara nodded at Bob, as he looked in her direction. "Mr. Whitney, how are you?"

"Just fine, Cara, thanks. I'll help Harry into the house." While he walked the old man up the steps, Laura explained to Cara in detail what had just occurred.

"So, a week from Thursday should be it."

Cara seemed somber.

"Are you all right?" Laura asked.

"I've got tons of people callin', so I can fill in the time just fine, but as crazy as it sounds, I'll miss the old coot."

"Cara, you've been the absolute greatest," Laura added, giving her a hug.

"I'm gonna miss Fridays the most, though," Cara replied; then turning to Laura she questioned, "You gonna be okay?"

"I think so, as long as I can still call and cry on your shoulder if I need to?"

"Anytime, darlin', anytime."

In the car on the way home from Harry's, Bob was

unusually quiet. The silence felt comfortable, so Laura waited for him to speak.

"I'm just glad we don't have to do that every day."

"Remember what Dr. Crosby said. He'll thank us, eventually."

"Thank us? He wanted to punch me, Laura. He said he wanted to kill me."

"Bob, you know he didn't know what he was saying. He was angry at everyone."

"Did you see the hatred in his eyes?"

"Bob, he hasn't always been that way. Don't you remember how he used to be?"

"I do remember, and honestly, sometimes I feel cheated."

"What do you mean?"

"I never had a dad I could talk to or go places with. He was never there for me. Now, when I try to help him, he says he wants to kill me. Damn him, why couldn't he have just been a decent father?"

Laura didn't know how to answer. She sat silent, letting him continue.

"I just don't want to turn out like him. It's like I'm angry but I pity him, all at the same time. How can that be?" He wanted to reach out and squeeze her hand, touch someone, but he couldn't, not with the way things were between them.

"Let's get him checked in, then give him a few days in the gold room. He'll be a new person. You'll see. It will be okay, Bob." Instinctively she reached over and clasped his fingers. She had not seen him this emotional in years—perhaps there was hope after all.

Laura was more optimistic than she had been in a long while; the incident at the nursing home had been terrible, but in many ways she wondered if it was a blessing. When her attorney called her at work three days later, she was shocked.

"Laura, this is Mitch Olsen. I just got a call from James Bagley, your husband's attorney. They're wondering if we can meet three weeks from next Friday to talk about the details of a final settlement. How will that work for you?"

She was confused. There must be some kind of mistake. When Bob had said good-bye just three days ago, they had held hands.

"There's a misunderstanding, Mitch. Bob was just here and—" She didn't want to go into the details but was sure this meeting must have been planned before last weekend.

"Jim said he'd just gotten off the phone with Bob."

"Let me get back to you," she mumbled.

She dialed Bob's home number first. When his machine picked up, she hung up and dialed his cell phone.

"Hello, this is Bob."

"What about last weekend? Didn't it mean anything? Didn't you feel anything at all?"

"Laura? Whoa, that didn't take you long."

"Who are you? Don't you feel anything anymore?"

"I just think it would be better if we each moved on, Laura. I appreciate what you're trying to do, but it's over."

"Appreciate it? You appreciate it?" Laura was raising her voice. "Are you serious? Harry was right, you really are a good for nothing son." With that, she slammed down the phone.

Several of the agents in the office stared, others pretended nothing had happened. Grant Midgley was the only one who headed toward her desk to see if he could help. But before he could make it across the room, she snatched her purse and bolted out the front door.

CHAPTER *Seven*

E WATCHED HER FROM AFAR BEFORE APPROACHING. IT was hard to tell, but she seemed to be waiting for him.

"Hi, Cynthia."

"Hey, Bob. You just starting or ending?"

"If I'm ending, I didn't run hard enough."

She laughed as he pointed to his dry shirt.

"You want to run together?" she asked.

"That'd be great."

She was wearing blue shorts today with a T-shirt and sports bra. "How's the pharmaceutical business these days?" she asked, making small talk.

"Terrific. Especially if you could get Brightman to prescribe more of our products."

"Always a salesman," she added. He took it as a compliment. "So how long have you lived in San Diego?" she questioned.

"About three or four months now, and I love it."

"I grew up in Santa Monica. It's hard to move away from the beach, if you're used to it." He was running at his usual pace and she seemed to keep up just fine. "What brought you to California?" she asked.

"My job, of course. This is a great territory. When the company offered me this region, I jumped at the chance."

"You were a drug rep before?"

"Yeah."

She was hoping he'd bring it up, but when he didn't, she asked directly.

"Married or single?"

"Well—yes." His reply caused her to laugh.

"That sounds like something a guy would say."

"I'm still married, but we're getting a divorce. It's not final yet . . ." They were the words she wanted to hear.

She continued before he had a chance to finish. "Sorry it didn't work out. I've been through one myself."

"I hear it's been going around," he added. She smiled. He continued, "How long have you been divorced? If you don't mind my asking?"

"Two years now," she replied.

"Kids?"

"I have a little girl, Breann. She's four. You?"

"Same here, only she's six, no, wait, seven, and her name's Emily." Nearing the pier he slowed to a stop. He was sweating and pulled off his shirt. She tried not to stare.

"How you doing? You want to walk back?" he inquired.

"Not yet, I'm still good." She took off at a slow run and he followed. He was surprised by her fitness.

"Have you been working for Mike a long time?"

"Almost two years."

They continued their friendly chat until they arrived back where they'd started.

"You want to go down to the point now?" he questioned.

"Thanks, but I think I'm done."

"Oh, okay . . ." Bob stumbled over what to say next. It didn't matter; she took over.

"It was a pleasure, Bob. Let's do it again."

"Thanks, that'd be great. Tomorrow?" He was trying to be funny but she answered immediately.

"Great, I'll see you tomorrow." She turned, waved, and jogged up the path toward the street.

It felt funny, almost like high school again. One thing for sure—he'd better not let Laura find out until after the divorce was final.

When Cara arrived, Harry was still in bed. It was nine-thirty before she heard the toilet flush. She tried to chat with him when he entered the kitchen, but he refused to acknowledge she was there. She fixed his favorite breakfast: crackers spread with butter and a glass of buttermilk. An hour later she noticed the food had not been touched.

He sat motionless at the table until late in the morning, when she shooed him out to the porch. He perked up briefly in the afternoon and tried to use his computer, but being confused about how to access the files, he finally gave up. Instead, sitting on the living room couch, he stared out the window, as if expecting someone to arrive.

Cara had been caring for the elderly for four years now and had developed a knack for sensing their needs. She had a feeling that moving Harry to a full-service care facility was the best thing to do. He would soon require more help than she could provide. No question about it, Harry needed to be in a home.

After fixing dinner and then getting out his medications, she tried again to talk with him.

"Harry?" He sat on the couch pretending to watch TV. "Harry, I know you're pretendin' not to hear me, but try to listen. I'm gonna be an hour late or so in the mornin', so you'll find your milk in the fridge and the crackers in the cupboard. If you want somethin' more, I'll fix it when I get here." He still didn't move. "Do you need some help gettin' to bed?"

He spoke no words but waved his hand in her direction. She took it as a signal that he was okay on his own.

"Good-night, Harry. Remember, you can push your alarm button if there's an emergency, but don't push anything unless the house is burnin' down. Okay? Harry?" She shook her head and headed out the door in a pretended disgust.

After he heard the car drive away, he shuffled to the bedroom and removed his shirt. It took several minutes to undo the buttons. Next he moved to the bathroom sink, shaved his face, and combed his hair. He clicked off the light and retraced his steps to the bedroom. It was difficult to find his favorite shirt and black socks in the dim light. He needed to be ready when she came. Once he was finished dressing and everything on his desk had been straightened, he headed off to bed.

CHAPTER *Eight*

$\mathcal{T}$HE ROOM WAS DECORATED WITH DOZENS OF COLORED leaves, created by placing copy paper over large maple leaves and then rubbing a crayon over the top. It was, after all, ecology month.

"Who knows where paper comes from—anyone?" Emily raised her hand. "Let's see—Emily, do you know the answer?"

"Trees. Paper's made out of trees."

"That's absolutely correct." As the teacher continued her lesson, the door opened and the principal stepped into the classroom. He hurried over to whisper something into Mrs. Cavenaugh's ear and then, turning toward the class, addressed Emily directly.

"Emily, if you could come with me to the office, your mother is here to pick you up."

"And don't forget your backpack," Mrs. Cavenaugh added.

Emily followed the principal down the hall. As she stepped into the office, her mother, who had been waiting in a chair, stood. Emily could see she'd been crying.

"Hi, honey," Laura whispered.

"What's wrong?" she questioned.

"Let's walk to the car and I'll tell you all about it."

She took her little girl by the hand, nodded to the office secretary, and headed out the door. They walked down the hall and almost to the doors before Laura spoke. This would be difficult. She decided they needed to sit, so they moved outside to the bench located just beyond the entrance.

"You know how Cara helps out Grandpa Whitney?" Emily nodded. "When she got there this morning, Grandpa was very sick. She called an ambulance and they took him to the hospital, but because he was old and not feeling well— honey, he passed away on the way there." Laura's eyes were watery as she spoke. "Emily, do you understand what I'm telling you?" Emily sat silent for just a few seconds, contemplating her mother's words. Then, as she grabbed her mother around the neck and hugged her tightly, she began to sob.

All Laura could do was hold her close and let her cry. After a few seconds, Emily pulled away and through her tears declared, "Mommy, last time I was at Grandpa's I said I didn't want to play there anymore. I didn't mean it—I didn't really mean it."

Tears streamed down both their cheeks as Laura hugged her weeping daughter.

"I know, baby, and he knows too. He loved you so much. It wasn't your fault."

They huddled together on the school bench for several minutes before getting up and walking hand in hand to the car.

Laura had rushed to the hospital before picking up Emily at school. Cara had reached her on the cell phone after calling the ambulance. She drove straight to the emergency room but was still too late; they had tried to revive Harry in the ambulance, but said he had technically passed away at home. The death certificate read "natural causes."

"It appears he simply stopped breathing. Very common among old people. It happens all the time," the doctor assured her.

The doctor had called Bob to inform him of Harry's passing before Laura had arrived at the hospital. Before leaving to pick up Emily from school, Laura opened her cell phone and dialed his number; he didn't answer. Once they got home and Emily was settled down watching TV, Laura walked upstairs and dialed his number again. She felt guilty now for losing her temper the last time they'd talked.

"Bob Whitney."

"Bob, it's Laura. Are you all right?"

"I'm fine, Laura. How's Emily?" He seemed somber but sounded okay.

"She cried for a while but we've had a long talk and she seems to be doing better. Are you really okay?"

"Me? I'm fine," he replied.

"Really?" she insisted. She was surprised he wasn't more distraught. She knew they'd never been close, but after all, Harry was his father. "Are you really okay?"

"Now you're sounding like our marriage therapist."

"I'm glad to hear you're taking the news so well, Bob."

"Listen, the six o'clock flight is booked, so I'm coming in on the nine. I didn't know whether—" He paused.

At first she hesitated, but then, remembering Emily, she agreed. "Yes, you should stay here, Bob. Emily will need all the support we can give her. We have to wait to tell her about us, though. The poor girl doesn't need to deal with two traumas in one week."

"You're right, Laura, and thanks."

"Do you need me to pick you up?"

"No, you stay with Emily. I'll get a rental car."

"See you tonight."

"Good-bye."

The funeral was held in the large redbrick church near Harry's house. It was a beautiful service with dozens of friends in the neighborhood attending. After moving to the cemetery for a brief graveside prayer, several friends and family members returned to the church's meeting hall for a luncheon provided by some of the women of the congregation. In addition to Bob, his older sister, Michelle, and their families, a number of distant relatives attended.

As Bob watched his sister now from across the table, he realized they had hardly had a chance to visit, at least not without a crowd standing around. She and her husband had arrived late the night before and opted to stay in a hotel by the airport. It looked to Bob like she had put on weight, and he wondered how she was getting along with Greg. She was three years older than Bob and had married early, at nineteen, to Greg Bradley. Their attraction to each other wasn't surprising to Bob; the timing was. They had met when Greg had just been accepted to graduate school in New York. Six weeks later Michelle had left a note telling Harry she and

Greg had gone off to get married. Harry had been furious. He had refused to speak with her for almost a year. Though they'd finally reconciled, their relationship had never seemed the same. Bob had predicted his sister's marriage wouldn't last, but twenty years later they still seemed happy. It was more than he could say for his own marriage, he realized.

Bob knew it had been difficult for Michelle to live so far away. She and Greg and their two sons usually came for a visit at Christmas. Greg didn't like to stay long, so their visits were always kept short. This time they had come alone, deciding it best to leave their boys at home. Michelle had mentioned earlier that Greg had to be back for work in the morning, and so they were catching the early flight. Now, with Harry gone, Bob wondered if he'd see much of his sister anymore.

Greg had worked at a brokerage firm in New York for several years but had recently taken a job in Boston. No question they would stay put on the East Coast. Everyone knew they were doing well financially, as Greg was sure to bring it up. He was a nice enough guy, just overly proud of what he had accomplished. Bob found it worked best to simply ignore his bragging.

As the luncheon started to break up, Bob walked to the corner of the large church hall, where he noticed Michelle standing by herself. Growing up, they had always been close. Now that they stood alone together, he found surprisingly little to say.

"It was a great service, wasn't it?"

She nodded thoughtfully. "I will miss him."

He wished he could answer that he would miss Harry too. He hated admitting that he felt nothing at all. Instead, he listened quietly as she continued.

"I mean, I can't say we ever got along. He was always so obstinate. It's funny though, when you called, telling me he'd passed away, I sat down on the kitchen floor and cried."

"You get it from him."

"My emotion?"

"No, your obstinacy."

She smiled at Bob's quip. "Always a joker when emotions run high, aren't you?"

Bob shrugged. "It's easy to joke. We're talking about Harry here," he responded.

"I do remember quite a few good times, you know, before I left to get married. He wasn't Father of the Year, but I think he did the best he could under the circumstances."

"Yeah, sure, I guess so," Bob replied.

"I don't want to remember Dad as a grouchy old man. I'd rather think back to better times."

"There were better times?"

She ignored his remark. "So, how are you and Laura doing?"

"Fine."

"Really? You wouldn't fib to your sister, would you?"

He paused, watching her study his face. "No, not really. It looks like it's over. It's just not the same anymore." She could see this time he was serious.

"I'm sorry, Bob—really sorry. We've been through some rough times as well, Greg and I. In fact, you ought to see us get into a shouting match. It's quite a sight. I'm not sure why, but for some reason, we seem to get through it. Are you sure there aren't still times she takes your breath away?"

"More like she sucks the life right out of me."

"It's that bad?"

"I just feel emptiness most of the time. Like there's nothing there anymore. Not like years ago."

"So, what's changed?"

"We've been trying to figure that out. So far no answers."

"We'll, I'd lecture you, little brother, if I thought it would help."

Greg joined them. He reached over and put his arm around Bob as if they'd been good friends all of their lives. Michelle excused herself, leaving the men alone.

"So sorry, Bob. My condolences," Greg began.

"Thanks."

"Nice service, though. Lots of people showed up."

"Yes, that's important," Bob replied. Greg didn't seem to notice the sarcasm in his voice.

"Always a nice old man."

"Nice?"

There was an obvious pause before Greg continued.

"So, I guess you'll have to get the house cleaned up in order to sell it?"

Bob had guessed Greg would be the first to bring up Harry's assets. Like he needed the money. And bringing it up at the funeral—what a callous jerk.

"Yes, we do need to get the house cleaned out. I have to go back to San Diego, but I'll be back next week. Perhaps it's something we can get wrapped up then. Since Laura is an agent, at least we'll save on the commission." He expected that would brighten Greg's day.

"Hey, excellent idea. I hadn't thought of that."

"I still need to find out if Harry had a will and then talk to my attorney about how to handle things. I haven't had time yet, of course."

"No, of course not."

"I understand you have to get back to work right away as well? Flight leaving tonight?"

"Early in the morning. I'm telling you, Bob, at the rate companies are merging today, it's surprising I get any sleep. We're in the middle of preparing papers for two large banks. I can't say which ones, but when it hits the news, it will be big. Billions of dollars changing hands. I just wish my tiny percentage was bigger. But hey, the broker always gets the short end of the stick. We've got one deal in the office now where . . ." Bob wanted to reach out and turn off the switch. If only there were one. Instead he nodded, pretending to listen, while his mind drifted to other things.

Emily had endured the funeral well. Just a few tears. She was so adorable. He did need to get her out to San Diego for a visit, so they could spend some quality time together. Perhaps even before they sat her down and told her about the divorce, to prepare her just a bit for the news. She would love the beach. There was nothing better than a calm day at the beach in San Diego.

"So, you're still in San Diego?"

They would spend the day there and then perhaps go out for Mexican food at La Casita. Best enchiladas this side of Mexico City.

"You're still in San Diego?" Greg had raised his voice so half the room could hear.

Bob snapped out of his daydream.

"Yes, Greg, I am." Bob lowered his voice, hoping Greg would follow suit.

"It's a shame it isn't working out with you and Laura."

"Yes, it is," Bob whispered. "Well, I'd better see how Emily's holding up." With that, Bob excused himself and headed across the room toward Laura and his daughter.

"Hey, babe, will you take me outside to get some fresh air? I sure need some."

"Sure, Daddy." She reached up and took him by the hand.

Laura rested quietly beside Emily on her bed until she was sure she was asleep. She then tiptoed from the room, moved to the kitchen, poured a glass of milk and sat at the table.

She was exhausted physically, but her mind wouldn't stop. While she pondered the day's events, Bob stuck his head in the door.

"Guess I'll go to bed. Good-night, Laura."

"Why don't you love me anymore, Bob?" she asked vacantly.

"Laura, don't. It's been an emotional day for everyone. Let's just leave it there for now."

"I know it's over. I accept that now. I just don't want to go through life guessing, always wondering, so why, Bob? What is it? Is there someone else?"

"No, of course not."

"What, then?"

He hesitated, not wanting to continue but feeling obligated to try. "I don't think I can explain it. I just don't feel anything there anymore. It's not like it was. I don't know why or how, and you're not to blame. I just know I need to move forward." She looked puzzled so he continued. "Have you ever been somewhere and sat for so long that your legs got all jittery—but there were people around and you couldn't get up—and so you sat there going crazy, thinking you were going to scream, until finally it got so bad you just had to stand up and move around and shake your legs, no matter who was watching or what was going on around you? Well, that's how I feel."

Laura stared blankly. "You're leaving 'cause your legs are jittery?"

"Laura, I'm trying to explain."

"I'm trying to understand. I don't. When are we going to tell Emily?"

"We better wait until the next time I come to town or the time after, whatever you think is best."

"It's going to break her heart, Bob."

"Laura, don't you think I realize that? It breaks mine just thinking about her. It's just something I need to do."

She was too tired and confused to try to understand. He was about to leave when she spoke again.

"Don't you find it peculiar that he died, Bob, the day before we were supposed to move him to WestRidge?"

"What are you saying? That he willed himself to die?"

"You saw how he acted the day we took him there. Think about it. He's lived in the same house for fifty-something years. He could have moved, but never wanted to. He built the house himself and yes, I think he wanted to die there. I don't understand how, it just seems like too much of a coincidence to be anything else."

Bob doubted what she was saying, but it seemed pointless to discuss it. It simply didn't matter. The easiest thing to do was change the subject.

"Greg was wondering about the house. Can you believe him? I told him we'd get to it next week. I know Harry got his social security check each month. I guess he must have some other money saved as well."

"It strikes me as funny, how very little you seem to know about your father."

"Remember, we weren't exactly buddies. I wonder what happens if there's no will? I have no idea how to take care of his affairs. I'll need to call my attorney and ask." The words *my attorney* grated on Laura, but she stayed silent as he continued. "I fly back to San Diego tomorrow afternoon, but I can come out for a few days the week after to clean out his house. Let's run over there in the morning and see how much work it will take to get it ready to sell, so we have an idea. Let's go that far, then we'll sit down and decide what to tell Emily. What do you say?"

There was no hug, no quick squeeze of the hand, no glance. Laura nodded, then both mouthed the words *goodnight* as they wandered to their own beds. As she tried to sleep, cold and alone with Bob downstairs, Laura couldn't get the thought out of her head. Can a person really will himself to die?

CHAPTER *Nine*

*A*FTER EMILY LEFT TO CATCH THE SCHOOL BUS, BOB AND Laura headed to Harry's house. It felt eerie. She kept expecting to see Cara or Harry come around the corner. Neither did. Bob went downstairs to look through the old wooden filing cabinets, while Laura wandered around upstairs. The furniture was still in great shape, but it was old. They could try to sell it in the classifieds, but she doubted they'd get much for it. It was odd to find the house so cold and empty. Harry was a hard man to understand, sometimes contemptible, often difficult, but he had his moments. It was sad to know he was gone; Emily's visits with him had become such a big part of their lives.

She wandered into the back bedroom where Harry had slept. On the floor by the desk, where he kept his computer, sat an open cardboard box. As she peered inside, Laura could see three large books stacked neatly on top of each other. Inquisitive, she pulled out the one on top and began to examine it closely. The pages were large, about the size of letter paper. They had been printed on just one side, and most appeared to have come from Harry's laser printer. The pages had holes punched in the left margins and were tied together with string, forming a book. The front and back covers were hard, apparently cut from wood and covered with an ivory-and-gold fabric. Twine held them together, creating a binding. Though the book was homemade, the workmanship was excellent. The title on the front cover had been penned in black ink. In the old man's familiar hand it read, "Poems of Life" by Harry Whitney.

She pulled the other two books out of the box and found them to be identical; each one containing poems and stories that Harry had apparently written.

As she opened a book and began to read the words more carefully, Bob's voice interrupted. "Laura, can you come down here? I found a will." Laura hurried down the steps, book in hand, to find Bob sitting in a chair next to the old cabinets. File drawers were open with folders spread on the floor. Bob was scanning several stapled pages he held in his hand. "Harry had a will all right. You're not going to believe this, but Harry left the house to Emily."

"To Emily?"

"That's what this says." He waved the papers in his hand. "This looks like it was written a year and a half ago. Boy, is Greg going to love this," he added with a mischievous grin.

"What else does it say?"

"It looks pretty standard from what I can tell. He leaves the house in a trust to Emily and the money in his savings account to Michelle's kids. There might be more recent bank statements in his desk upstairs, but from those filed down here, it looks like he has about fourteen thousand dollars in his savings. Yep, they're gonna be mad all right."

"Do you think it's legal?" Laura wondered.

"It's written by a lawyer, so I imagine it is. I don't know if a copy was ever filed with the state, but I'll take one to my attorney and have him check it out. We better not call Michelle and Greg until we know for sure."

"You aren't going to believe what I found either," Laura chimed in, handing her prize to Bob.

"What's this?" he replied, taking the book from her hand.

"Your dad wrote it, and then must have bound it himself. He was a pretty good craftsman in his time. It looks like poems and stories he's written over the years. Look at how well it's made."

Bob examined the book, surprised Harry could have done such a thing.

"Interesting. I'll have to read through it later." He set the book down on the desk next to the stacks of files.

"Bob, there are three of them, all exactly the same. I think we should take one to Emily. We can send the last one to Michelle and Greg."

"Sure, that sounds like a good idea," Bob replied, as he turned his attention back to the papers on the desk.

She left him to continue sifting through the files while she moved back upstairs. She found a chair to sit on, picked up one of Harry's books, and began to read. The poems were sometimes whimsical, sometimes serious; some made no sense at all. It's a shame what Alzheimer's will do to your mind and body, she thought. It's just so sad to watch people get sick as they grow old.

When Bob came up the stairs, he was carrying a box full

of file folders. "I found statements from a money market account that show another twenty-two thousand dollars. There's also some stock in his retirement account worth another twelve thousand plus. That's a total of forty-eight thousand, but it still doesn't come close to the value of the house. It's interesting though; as I read the will, I found out the house is left to a trust in Emily's name. If I'm reading it correctly, the house can't be sold until she's eighteen. I'll get a legal opinion, just to be sure."

"Really? Why would he have done that?" she wondered.

"Who knows?" Bob raised his eyebrows. "Who could ever figure the old man out."

"Do you have your book?"

"Oh, I left it downstairs. Just a second." Retracing his steps, Bob grabbed Harry's book of poems. He took it upstairs, placed it on top of the box of files, and carried them to the trunk of the car.

Laura told Grant Midgley that she had an appointment to show a house, but instead she drove to the city library. She was not sure where to start, so she approached the librarian at the information counter. "Hi, I'm doing some research into—well—death, and I'm wondering where to find books on that subject."

"Could you be a little more specific?"

Laura attempted a smile. "Okay, I'm wondering if a person can will himself to die?" She expected the woman to look at her as if she were crazy. Instead, the librarian turned warm and friendly.

"My brother died suddenly, so I understand. Let's see— the first place to start would be—" She punched several keys on the computer and then jotted down the references.

"Check these titles in the religion and philosophy sections, and then these in the medical reference area."

"I appreciate your help."

"Not at all. Let me know if you need anything else."

Laura headed to the religion and philosophy section first. There were two full aisles of books. She had hoped to find quick answers, but forty-five minutes later she found herself buried in a mountain of information about strange existential experiences. The second aisle contained scores of books about life after death, but nothing that addressed her question specifically. She was running short on time, so she headed to the medical reference area. She browsed rapidly, hoping to narrow her search, but most of the material seemed clinical. Just as she was about to give up, a section in one of the books caught her attention.

"Alzheimer's, Also Known as AD—Attacking the Elderly." She turned to the chapter and began to scan the information curiously.

"Alzheimer's disease is a progressive, neurodegenerative disease characterized by memory loss, language deterioration, poor judgement, and indifferent attitude. Appearing first as memory decline, over several years it destroys cognition, personality, and the ability to function. People with AD are eventually unable to care for themselves. The early symptoms of AD can easily be missed as they resemble natural signs of aging. Often similar symptoms can result from fatigue, grief, depression, illness, vision loss, and the use of alcohol.

The exact cause of AD is still unknown. Researchers believe it is due to a combination of genetic factors, the aging process, and the environment. An estimated four million people in the United States suffer from AD."

It was peculiar. It was known that Harry had AD, yet,

according to this article, his symptoms didn't quite fit. If it was a progressive disease, with conditions getting worse, why did Harry seem normal at times? Even up until the day they visited the rest home, there were moments, small moments, when he appeared to be coherent. As she scanned the article again, one particular sentence seemed to glare. "Similar symptoms can result from fatigue, grief, depression, illness. . . ." Was it possible Harry had had something besides Alzheimer's?

She copied the article on the machine and replaced the book on the shelf. Then, picking up her cell phone, she dialed Cara.

"Cara, hi, it's Laura."

"Hey, honey, how are you?"

"I'm fine. Thanks so much for coming to the funeral."

"Don't thank me for that. I had to say good-bye."

"You're priceless. I need to ask you a question."

"Sure, what's up?"

"Did you ever take Harry to the clinic?"

"Sure, a couple of times. The one on Highland Drive?"

"Yes. Do you remember the name of the doctor he would see?"

"No, I'd just wait outside. They tryin' to bill you for somethin'?"

"No, I just had a few questions."

"There's a whole bunch of doctors there. I bet though, if you swung by, someone there could tell you."

"Good idea. You want to go to lunch next week?"

"Sure. Give me a ring Monday and we'll figure it out."

After they said their good-byes, Laura picked up the phone book, looked up the number, and dialed the clinic. The receptionist answered on the sixth ring.

"TSI Medicare Clinic, please hold." It took nearly five minutes before she picked up again. "Thanks for holding, how may I help you?"

"I'd like to make an appointment to come in and talk to the doctor who saw Harry Whitney."

"Which doctor would that be?"

"I have no idea, that's why I'm calling."

"Just a moment."

Laura held for several more minutes waiting for the receptionist to return once again.

"Did you need to set up an appointment for Mr. Whitney?"

"Well no, Harry, I mean Mr. Whitney, passed away. I just have a couple of questions I'd like to ask the doctor."

"Just a minute, please." Ain't Medicare wonderful, Laura thought as she listened once again to the static-filled music through the phone.

"Ma'am, the doctor can't see you unless the patient gives his consent."

"But the patient is dead."

"I'm sorry. If you'd like to come by and fill out a waiver form, the doctor will review it."

"Did you hear me? The patient is dead," she protested.

"I heard you, ma'am. That's why a waiver form needs to be filled out."

"I'll be right down." She'd heard of bureaucracy, but this was ridiculous. Knowing she stood a better chance with a warm body, face-to-face, she drove straight to the clinic. After an initial chat with the receptionist, the same one who had answered the phone, Laura was convinced the woman had no warm blood in her at all.

"So, let me get this straight. You need the patient's signature, but I can't get that because he's dead. If he were alive, then I wouldn't need his signature to find out why he died, because he'd still be alive. Is that right?"

"Ma'am, I've only been here a month. I don't make the rules."

"Let me take a wild guess. You were transferred from the Department of Motor Vehicles? Am I right?"

The woman didn't even smile. "No, ma'am. I came from Toxicology."

"Is there a doctor, any doctor I can speak with?"

"I'm sorry, but not without an appointment."

"Great! I'd like to make an appointment then."

"What's your patient number?"

"I don't have one."

"I'm sorry, but you need a patient number in order to make an appointment."

"Do you realize how ridiculous you people are?"

"Ma'am, please, I don't make the rules."

"Ridiculous!" Laura repeated as she turned in her fury and stormed out of the office. Just before the elevator doors closed, a man in a white coat rushed on and held out his hand.

"Hi, I'm Dr. Iverly." Laura shook his hand without saying a word. "I couldn't help overhearing. Can I help you with something?"

"Do you realize you work with a bunch of idiots?" He was only trying to help and as the words came out, she regretted her harshness. He didn't seem to mind.

"Tell me about it," he answered with a smile. "What can I do for you?"

She took a deep breath. "First, thank you."

"Glad to help."

"My father-in-law, Harry Whitney, came here. He just passed away from Alzheimer's and I had a few questions."

The elevator doors opened. They stepped out into the hall to continue talking.

"Once a patient has died, we're not allowed to give out any information; it has to do with malpractice and lawsuits, but if you keep it quiet, I'll check it out and call you—off the record, of course."

She was shocked. Amid the swirling sea of bureaucracy, pools of sanity managed to survive. "That would be a gift from heaven."

"No problem. What do you want to know?"

"Did he have it? Alzheimer's, I mean."

"Is that it?"

"Basically, yes. Let me know if he suffered from anything else—other symptoms, that sort of thing."

"Okay, tell me his name again."

"It's Harry. Harry Whitney." He jotted the name down in his pad.

"And now, if you'd give me your phone number." He waited, pen in hand.

"My what?" His question felt intrusive and out of place.

"Your phone number. I'd like your phone number so I can call and let you know what I find out."

She was embarrassed. "Yes, of course. Sorry." She repeated her number while the doctor noted it on the paper.

"And your name again?"

"Laura. Laura Whitney."

"Terrific, I'll call you tonight. Will you be home?"

"I will."

"Then we'll talk tonight." She turned and walked toward the parking garage. He waved as she walked away.

"I'm not sure if I was just helped, or hit on," she mused to herself with a grin.

She was in the shower and didn't hear the phone ringing. Emily was supposed to be in bed, but yelled through the door.

"Mom, there's a man on the phone who wants to talk to you."

"Coming, coming. Thanks, dear, now go climb in bed right this instant." Emily rolled her eyes, giving Laura the "it wasn't my phone call" look before running back to her room.

"Hello, this is Laura."

"Hi, Laura. This is Dr. Iverly. Was that your daughter?" The question caught her off guard. At first she was sorry the call woke Emily up, but suddenly she was grateful.

"Why, yes. That was my seven-year-old daughter, Emily."

"She said you were in the shower. Sorry to disturb you." Laura would have to have a little discussion about phone etiquette with Emily, first thing in the morning.

"Uh—no trouble. What did you find out?"

"I checked his file. It's pretty standard stuff. Remember, with Medicare, they don't do extensive testing."

"So did he have Alzheimer's?"

"The file says he did, but honestly, there's no way of knowing for sure now that he's deceased. He had all the symptoms, but so do a high percentage of elderly people. The only thing that struck me as peculiar was that according to the notes, he was always quite coherent during his visits— relatively speaking. The disease would have to have been in its early stages. It wouldn't be fatal until it moved into its more advanced stages."

"So, Dr. Iverly, let me get this straight . . ."

"Please, call me Steve."

"Okay, Dr. Steve. If a patient has Alzheimer's would he ever be coherent? Would he have times each day where he was normal—mentally, I mean?"

"It's a progressive disease so in its early stages someone with the disease would appear to be normal. But as the disease develops most physical and mental abilities diminish progressively until the patient is essentially helpless."

"Do you believe Harry had Alzheimer's?"

"Again, it's hard to say."

"Let's say he didn't. What else would cause his symptoms?"

"Did he drink?"

"Not very often."

"Well, there is another possibility, but it's not my specialty." He paused.

"What? What is it?"

"Just a hunch, but it could be he was suffering from a mental illness."

"You think he could have been crazy?"

"That's not exactly the medical term."

"What do you mean then?"

"He had the classical symptoms for Alzheimer's. That would be the easy diagnosis and the one that would—how shall I say this—give the clinic the best return. But a mental illness, say a form of depression, could also produce the symptoms you've described. I would suggest you find a specialist and run it by him or her. Perhaps they'd be able to shed some light on it for you."

"Can I ask you one last question?"

"Certainly."

"Can a person will themselves to die?"

"At a specific time? Not that I know of. I've seen studies that show how a patient's attitude will influence his recovery. That's to say, a higher percentage of patients who want to live will recover over those with the very same disease who don't care or are despondent. So, to answer your question, attitude is certainly important. But as far as wishing to die, say tomorrow, and having it happen—I haven't seen it."

"Doctor?"

"Yes?"

"I do appreciate what you've done for me."

"No problem. You take care of Emily and if you need anything else, give me a call."

This was a nice guy. "Okay, thanks."

The instant she hung up the phone, it rang again.

"Laura, this is Bob. Your phone's been busy forever. Who have you been talking to?"

"Steve Iverly."

"Who? Oh, never mind. Listen, I can't come tomorrow. You know, to start cleaning out Dad's house. Things have come up. I'd like to do it toward the end of next week. Will that work? After all, it's not like we're going to sell it before then anyway."

"That should be fine. My schedule is pretty flexible."

"That's great. My attorney's checking into the will. From a quick look at it, he said he believes we can sell the house after all. The money from the sale simply has to stay with the trust until Emily turns of legal age. I should know all the details in a few days."

"Bob, before you go, I did some research. Did you know that Alzheimer's or AD attacks the nerves in the brain? Most people start by forgetting small stuff, but by the time it works into its final stages, they're essentially helpless."

"What's your point?"

"Well, it wasn't that way with Harry. I mean he'd have times where he'd forget things or be mean, but he'd still have times where he could think fine. It doesn't quite fit."

"Laura?"

"Yes?"

"Don't take this personally, but forget about it. Harry's dead. It doesn't matter. Let him rest in peace."

"Look, I'm sorry for caring, but it just seems strange to me, that's all."

"It's funny. He's my dad, and you're the one who's concerned."

"I agree, Bob. That is strange."

He knew she was right. "Please, don't make it worse on Emily," he continued.

"And I guess you're the expert on making the situation good for Emily?"

"I'd better go, this is getting ridiculous. I'll call you when I find out my schedule for next week. Bye."

Though Laura heard the click as Bob hung up, she continued to hold the phone against her ear. She wasn't angry at his quick departure, simply frustrated that he wouldn't listen, that he didn't care. Couldn't he see that something about his father's death wasn't right?

As she slowly hung up the receiver, she continued to wonder about Harry.

CHAPTER Ten

THE RESTAURANT WAS AUTHENTIC ENOUGH. CHEAP SPEAK-
ers screwed into the ceiling played mariachi music; colorful
paintings adorned the walls; and the smell of cilantro and
salsa filled the air. It wasn't extravagant. It wasn't even
charming, but customers didn't come to La Casita for
atmosphere; they came because the food was incredible. He
had already worked his way through two glasses of water
and half a bowl of chips by the time she arrived. It seemed
harmless enough to meet her here. It was not like a true date
where they drove together. As she approached, he noticed
her hair was down, falling over her shoulders, not pulled
back the way she wore it when they jogged. She was friendly
and cute and most of all, she was interested. He couldn't,
after all, spend the rest of his days alone just because things
with Laura weren't working out. They'd jogged together on
several occasions, and now it seemed time to take the next

step. It was a big step and it made him nervous. It was scary and yet thrilling, all at the same time.

"Cynthia, hi."

"Hey, Bob. Sorry I'm late." She stepped toward him, giving him a quick hug before sitting down.

"You're not late. I just got here myself." She smiled, her gaze turning to the half-eaten bowl of chips in the middle of the table. "Have you been here before?" he questioned.

"I drive by all the time but never imagined actually eating here."

"Order the chicken enchiladas and you'll never want to leave. You'll quit at Brightman's office and waitress here, just so you can eat them all day."

"My, they must be good."

"Trust me. There are times I take some home and then eat them for breakfast the next day."

She laughed. "You eat them for breakfast?"

"They're that good. Trust me."

"Trust me? If I only had a dollar for every time a guy said that to me, I could buy La Casita. In fact, I could buy the whole chain."

Their conversation continued pleasantly through dinner. When the food arrived, she agreed it was terrific. He found her attractive and charming, and he got the impression she felt the same about him. They chatted a bit, sipping coffee, before Bob laid down his credit card to pay the bill.

"And you know the best part?"

"No, what's that?"

"Since you work for Dr. Brightman, I get to write this meal off."

She rolled her eyes. After signing the slip, they walked

slowly to the entrance. She paused, letting him open the door for her. Once out front on the sidewalk, both stood silent—another one of those uncomfortable moments.

Cynthia finally spoke. "I have to admit, the food was wonderful. I don't think I'd eat it for breakfast though, but overall I'd say definitely the best Mexican food I've had."

"Yeah, I'd eat there every night if it wasn't for the mariachi music. I think they play it just to keep the crowds moving through."

"Hey, listen Bob," she interrupted. "I live pretty close. You want to come over to my place—you know—for a drink?"

He hesitated for only a moment. "Um—sure. I could do that."

"I don't want to force you," she prodded with a smile.

"Not at all—I'd love to."

Her apartment was nearby and the evening air was pleasant, so Bob left his car parked at the restaurant and they walked. As they reached the front door, she slipped the key into the lock and turned it slightly, letting him push open the door. Just inside, a familiar beep sounded from her purse. She looked frustrated. "Sorry. It's always at the worst times." Pulling the beeper from her purse, she studied the number. "Sure enough. I work two nights a month at nighttime pediatrics. Wouldn't you know they'd beep me tonight."

"Don't worry about it. We'll do it some other time."

"Sorry. Can I give you a lift back to your car?"

"Thanks, but it's such a great night, I think I'll walk. I enjoyed dinner."

"It was very nice. Hey, I think we could use some more samples at the office. Drop in this week?"

"I'll plan on it."

❖ ❖ ❖ ❖

It had been two weeks since the funeral, long enough that Laura was now able to discuss Harry with Emily and not get teary eyed. Bob had put off coming back to take care of Harry's affairs twice. It suited her just fine. The longer it took, the longer she'd have before she had to break Emily's heart again.

"Mommy, read me a bedtime story."

"Oh honey, it's so late. Can't we just read one in the morning?"

"Huh? Why would you read a bedtime story in the morning? That don't make no sense at all."

"Doesn't make sense," she corrected.

"You're right, so just read it now." She giggled as Laura eyed her warily, not sure if she was being manipulated by cunning or innocence.

"All right, babe, but just one." Picking up a Dr. Seuss book from the dresser, she plopped down on the bed next to her daughter.

"Mommy, not that one," Emily moaned. "We read that one last time."

"Well, then you pick one, but hurry."

"I know." Emily's eyes lit up. She jumped out of bed and ran to the dresser. She reached up on her tallest tippy-toes and pulled Harry's book down from the shelf.

"Really?" Laura questioned. "You want to read that one?"

"Sure, Mommy. Grandpa wrote it."

"I know, but it doesn't make any sense, especially to a seven-year-old."

"Please, please, please," she pleaded, batting the eyelashes on her big brown eyes.

"All right, but just one," Laura conceded. Opening the book to the first poem, she began to read.

Ergaldy Mergaldy, I Laughingly Yammer,
The hidden enigma, puzzle and stammer
Silly worgle, of rhyming dawdler
It's special time forever after.

"Crazy old man sounds like Dr. Seuss on painkillers," Laura mumbled to herself. "I told you it wouldn't make any sense."

"I think it's funny, Mom. What does *igma* mean anyways?"

"It's *enigma,* dear. It means—well, it's something that's puzzling. It's just a nonsense poem, honey. The words aren't supposed to make sense. Your grandpa was sick and didn't know what he was writing all of the time. He just liked putting silly words together."

"I like it, Mom," she declared, staring at the strange words on the page. Then with a look of sheer joy she exclaimed, "Look Mommy, the funny words spell my name."

"What do you mean, honey?"

"The letters in the words on top—Grandpa spelled my name." Taking a second look at the nonsensical poem, Laura began pulling the first letter from each word.

E-M-I-L-Y. Her mouth dropped open. "Oh, my goodness!"

"What Mom, what is it?"

"It spells your name."

"That's what I told you," she repeated.

"No, I mean it really spells your name."

Emily giggled, delighted to have found her name in the poem before her mother did.

Laura continued through the poem, pulling out the first

letters and putting them together. *T-h-e P-a-s-s-w-o-r-d i-s t-f-a.* "Amazing," she mumbled. Laura thumbed through the other poems frantically. Pulling out first letters didn't seem to spell anything. She read several slowly but could see no other patterns or hidden meanings.

"You like them, Mom?" Laura didn't reply, consumed in the pages of the book. "Are you listening to me, Mom?"

"What? Oh, sure, baby." Laura rolled off the bed, bent over, and kissed Emily on the cheek. "You get some sleep. I'm going to go read through Grandpa's book some more in my bed. Good-night. I love you." She rushed out the door and headed for her bedroom.

Turning page after page, she scanned the words. Some were nonsense poems; others seemed more serious. Many were peculiar. Did others have hidden meanings, she wondered. When did he create this book? He didn't seem coherent enough to have done it recently. The password must be for a file on Harry's computer, she reasoned. Now she wished she'd brought it home. It was too late to get it tonight, but first thing in the morning she'd run over to his house.

At midnight she was still reading. She was intrigued that Harry had had the mental capacity to put such a book together. She picked up the phone and dialed Bob's number.

"Hello," he answered the phone quickly and sounded alert. She paused for a moment straining to hear any other voices with him. "Hello?" he repeated.

"Bob, it's Laura."

"Laura, what's up?"

"Did I wake you?"

"No, I was awake."

"Oh, then I'll call back later," she teased.

"Laura, it's twelve-fifteen. Is everything okay?"

"I don't think so. Have you got your dad's book of poems there?"

"What?"

"I said, have you got your dad's book of poems there? Get it quick."

"Are you really okay?"

"Now you're sounding like the therapist. Just get the book of poems, Bob!"

"Okay, okay, don't get so feisty, just a second." In the background she could hear him fumbling around trying to find the book.

"All right, I've got it."

"Open it to the first poem, read it, and tell me what you see."

"Do what?"

"Please, Bob, just read it."

"Just a minute." After several silent seconds, he continued, "I've read it. So what?"

"Do you see anything peculiar about the words?"

"Not really. Harry used to call me a silly worgle when I was little, but that's it. Why?"

"Don't call him Harry, he was your dad."

"Is there a point to all this, Laura?"

"What's an enigma, Bob?"

"I'm not really sure. What?"

"Where'd you go to school? It's a puzzle or a riddle. Never mind, just look at the first letter of each word—starting on the top line." She smiled, knowing the response she was about to get.

"Wait! Laura, there's a message in there. It spells *Emily*." A few seconds of silence passed. "But, what's the password for?"

"I'm not sure. I'm guessing there are files on your dad's computer."

"So you haven't been to Harry's yet?" he questioned.

"No, I'll swing by in the morning."

"Call me and let me know. Will you? Laura?" Without answering, she hung up the phone.

CHAPTER *Eleven*

LAURA AND EMILY AWOKE EARLY AND HEADED TO HARRY'S house before school. The house was still empty, but somehow it didn't feel as lonely this morning. They clicked on the light and trotted over to the computer to turn it on. The antiquated machine whirred for several minutes as the operating system loaded. Laura waited patiently until Windows flashed onto the screen.

"What you looking for, Mom?" Emily quizzed.

"I'm not sure, let's find out."

She scanned the hard drive for files, and sure enough, there was a folder called "Letters for Emily." She opened it, revealing the contents. Twenty-six files, each numbered consecutively, listed on the screen. They appeared to coincide with the table of contents in Harry's book—each poem, puzzle, or story having a number from one to twenty-six. She clicked on the first and waited for it to open. As she did, a small box requesting a password popped onto the screen.

"Perhaps the crazy old man wasn't so crazy after all," she whispered. Cautiously, she typed in the letters *tfa* and hit Enter. "Incorrect Password—Please Try Again." Confused, she opened the book and looked again at the words.

"E-m-i-l-y t-h-e p-a-s-s-w-o-r-d i-s . . ."

"Wait, I know." This time she typed in "time forever after" just as it was written in the poem, and then hit the Enter key once more. After the hard drive whirred again, the file opened before her on the screen.

"Yes!" she exclaimed, giving Emily a quick squeeze.

"What is it?"

"It looks like Grandpa wrote you a letter. Listen, I'll read it to you."

Dearest Emily,

You found the secret of the first poem. I knew you would, you're a smart girl!

As you may have guessed by now, each poem or story in my book has its own secret for you to discover. If you look hard, you will find each contains a password that will lead you back here to my letters.

I have done this for two reasons. First, I want to teach you that in life, the solutions to problems are not always clear. Often, you will need to look beneath the surface to find your answers.

The second reason is a more practical one that has to do with my condition. I fear as my symptoms worsen, I may accidentally delete or alter my work. The passwords help protect me from myself.

You are so young. You may wonder what an old man like me could teach? I wonder as well. I certainly don't claim to know all the answers. I'm barely figuring out the questions. I do know that I want you to have a better life than I have had. I want you to learn from the many mistakes I've made. Learn from the good times and the not-so-good times. For you see, this journey is a test and many of the problems that I have faced, you will face. Life has a strange way of repeating itself and I want my experience to help you. I want to make a difference.

My hope is that you'll consider my words and remember my heart. If you're helped even once, then my prayers will have been answered. Much of what I say may not make sense right away, but as you grow, perhaps it will be appreciated. Remember me for my words and my heart. Please forget the times I made you angry or sad. It is a wish that everyone should be granted.

My book of poems and these letters are my gift to you. I hope they bring you joy. I hope that as you read them, you will think of me, because I will be thinking of you.

Love,

Grandpa Harry

"That sly son of a . . ." Looking at Emily, she concluded with *gun.* "That sly son of a gun."

"He wrote me a letter!" Emily was thrilled.

"He sure did, babe. He wants to tell you how smart and wonderful you are."

"Are there more?"

"There are, but we have to find his secrets first. Sit down and I'll show you."

Sitting on the couch, Laura explained how the password Emily discovered was hidden in the poem; how every poem had one, and as they discovered each one, they could read more of Grandpa's letters.

"Can we show my letter to Dad?" Emily wondered.

"Absolutely." Walking to the computer, Laura clicked on the printer icon and waited for the page to drop from the printer. Once it had, she exited Windows and turned off the machine. She could copy the files, but not knowing what else might be hidden on Harry's hard drive, it seemed best to take the whole thing home.

As Laura moved behind the desk to unplug the monitor and printer cables, a cracking sounded beneath her feet. She jumped back and saw a small plastic prescription bottle in pieces on the carpet where she'd stood. Picking up the shattered container, she scanned the label. The doctor's name and address were different from that of the clinic she had visited on Highland Drive, yet the prescription had been filled recently. Peculiar. Emily was already late for school, so Laura pulled off the broken pieces of plastic and dropped the label into her purse. It took three trips, but after the computer was safely loaded in the car, she scooted Emily outside and locked the door.

Laura dropped Emily off at school and rushed to an appointment with a buyer. It was just after noon when she arrived home. The answering machine showed eight messages, seven of which were from Bob. Rather than returning his calls, Laura studied Harry's book while waiting for the phone to ring again. It didn't take long.

"Hello?" she answered slowly.

"Did you find something?"

"You should say hello first, Bob."

"Hello, did you find something?"

"Yes, we did." She paused, waiting for his response.

"What? You want me to beg?"

This was better than calling him at midnight, Laura thought. "Just like I guessed. He has a file on his computer for each of his poems. The password Emily found opened the first file."

Bob interrupted, "Emily found it?"

"You have a very smart daughter."

"You're right about that. So, what does the file say?"

"Is your fax machine on? I'll just fax it to you. Oh, there is one other thing."

"Yes?"

"I found an empty bottle of pills at your dad's, but they're not from the clinic he normally went to."

"So?"

"Don't you find that strange?"

"I don't know. It's probably an old bottle."

"It's not."

"You're beating a dead horse to death, Laura—excuse the pun."

"Don't you want to know all the answers?"

"Answers to what? That he was sick and died?"

"I know that Bob, but there's more going on here than just that. I can feel it. Wait until you read his letter."

"Will anything I say stop you from looking?"

The answer was simple. "Not until I find what I'm looking for."

"When you find Jimmy Hoffa, will you let me know?" She ignored his retort. He continued, "You'll fax the letter right now?"

"Only if you hang up the phone, Bob."

She wanted to wait. Instead she walked to the fax machine in the bedroom, slipped in the paper, and dialed his number.

After she had finished, she rifled through her purse and extracted the label from the prescription bottle. It was new. It made her angry that Bob wouldn't even listen. She scribbled the date of the prescription and the name of the drug on a piece of paper and circled the date boldly. Underneath she wrote just two words. "It's new!" She placed the sheet into the machine and faxed it to him as well.

After the fax finished, she picked up the phone and dialed the number of the pharmacy printed on the label. The pharmacist was polite and located the record quickly. The original prescription had been filled six years ago. It had been renewed a year and a half ago and had been written with five refills, the maximum allowed. The last one had been mailed out seven months earlier. For further questions, he recommended she call the doctor directly and gave her the number. The phone rang only once.

"Riley Medical, may I help you." To Laura's relief, the receptionist at this place sounded civil.

"Yes, is Dr. Jensen available, please?"

"He's just finishing up with a patient. May I have him return your call in a moment?"

"Yes, please. It's concerning my father-in-law, a patient of his, Harry Whitney."

"Did you say Harry?"

"Yes."

"Then he's a man?"

"Of course he's a man. I said he was my father-in-law."

"I'm sorry, Dr. Jensen is a gynecologist. You must be looking for Rodney Jensen, his father."

"That could be. The label just has an initial before the last name. Does he work there? Could I speak to him please?" There was no answer. "Hello? Could I speak to him please?"

"I'm sorry, ma'am, but Dr. Rodney Jensen passed away just over a year ago."

"What?" She was confused. "I'm sorry. I didn't know." She was about to hang up when an idea struck. "Could I speak to his son, as soon as he's free?"

"Certainly. Just a moment, please."

While she waited for the doctor, she stared again at the date on the tiny label she held in her hand.

CHAPTER Twelve

THE NEXT MORNING LAURA AWOKE EARLY. THE POEMS WERE perplexing, and one especially had her intrigued. Sitting at the kitchen table, waiting for Emily to wake up, she opened the book and again read the words.

Kathryn,
  Believe—and love will burst forth as rays of morning light.
  Touch—in moments unexpected, a world dark, now brilliant white.
  Warmth—love so wondrous, bequeathed from you to me.
  Both encircled at an instant—I was blind, you made me see.
  Apart but joined—first love you touched my very soul.
  Lost & blind, you gave sight—peace of mind—you made me whole.
              Love, Harry

Laura read the poem over several times. It was quirky, but that meant a clue was hidden inside—but where? She read the lines quickly and then slowly, sounding out each word carefully. . . . *both encircled—at an instant* . . . The phrase seemed peculiar. Shouldn't it be *in* an instant? She could tell she was on to something, but was not sure what. The poem was describing love, but what else . . . *both encircled—at an instant . . . apart but joined* . . .

The answer came bluntly, and after seeing it she felt foolish for taking so long. Picking up a pencil, she drew a light circle around the names of Kathryn and Harry in the poem. She spoke to him as if he were sitting by her side. "Okay, Harry, there you go. You're both *encircled.* You're apart, now let's get you *joined.*" As she talked, she drew a straight line between the circled names, linking words in the poem. She chuckled at his cleverness. It was so plain—and yet so beautiful. She read the words aloud that the line connected. "Believe in love at first sight." It was a long password, but there was no question this was the secret. She moved to the computer and clicked on the file. Her heart raced as she typed in the words. Harry wasn't just a crazy old man; behind the crusty façade was a real human being—a person who cared about his family. She hoped Bob would start to discover this as well.

As the words flashed upon the screen, she began to read.

Dearest Emily,

Love is a strange and wonderful thing. It makes you do things that you'd never even consider if you'd been thinking clearly. It's spontaneous and unpredictable, sheer misery and absolute bliss, all mixed as one.

In your life, Emily, you'll have your share of pain and heartache; but to balance that pain, you'll know the joy of love. *If you ask people about love, most will say you can only experience the full bloom of love after a life of sharing, affection, selfless giving, and mutual sacrifice. They are correct. Also know that the flower can begin to bloom the first time your eyes meet. I know because it happened to me.*

Let me tell you, Emily, the story of how your grandma Kathryn and I first met. Understand that if she were here today to defend herself, she would dispute what I am about to tell you as pure rubbish. But, as God is my witness, this is how it happened.

I was pitching at varsity baseball practice that Tuesday afternoon when she arrived. As I hurled balls over the plate, she entered the stands, strolled down the steps, and sauntered over to our team's bench. Her face was ravishing, her skin clear and smooth, her smile enchanting. The light reflected off of her auburn hair in such a way that I imagined her to be an angel from heaven sent to watch me practice. She had the softest brown eyes and as I watched her, I knew we were meant to be together. There was just one problem—she was holding hands at the time with my best friend, Bud Nobles.

Bud and I were rooming together at USC that semester. He had told me about a girl that he'd run into from Wharton, Texas, but I had yet to meet her. It was a cruel quirk of fate that he found her first, when he dropped by the school registrar's office to change his schedule. She had just been hired as a staff assistant and Bud had been her first "customer." Enchanted by her twangy Texas accent, he seized the moment and asked her to go to the Spring dance, then just days away. Because she was new to the school and didn't know any better, she agreed. Now, as fate would have it, I stood in the middle of the field, sweaty, dirty, and alone,

while Bud sat holding hands with the most wonderful crea-
ture I had ever seen.

It's a dangerous thing when a girl comes between two
best friends. I had watched it destroy friendships with oth-
ers and I wasn't going to let that happen to ours. Right
then and there, in the middle of the wet grass field at USC,
before I'd even spoken a word to her, I began to devise my
plan.

Wednesday at the dorm had been designated as "study"
night; to guys in college that meant poker. The game was
always the same, seven-card stud, no jokers, ten-dollar
limit, two-dollar maximum raise. Four of us played reli-
giously. Bud was thinking of skipping the game that next
night to ask Kathryn to a movie; I intercepted him after
English class, just in time. It wouldn't be fair to the group, I
pleaded. He had an obligation, a responsibility, and even a
duty, to show up and support the poker-playing men of the
world. He needed to carry on that sacred tradition person-
ally. In the end, he had no choice.

The game began right at nine. I was nervous and by ten,
just an hour later, I had lost half my stake. Since I knew this
to be my only chance, I closed my eyes and pictured the dim-
ples, the smile, those captivating eyes, the accent that would
make the strongest man's knees buckle like a newborn baby.
I vowed success and started my comeback.

The rules were set in stone; play until midnight; no bow-
ing out, even if you'd made a quick run. If you ran out of
money before midnight, you'd bet services; make beds for a
week, wash cars, that sort of thing. At eleven forty-five I was
on a roll, Bud was tapped out, and I knew it was time to
make my move. It was my deal. After a few initial rounds of
small betting, I dealt the last card of each hand to the players.

I showed two jacks, a six and a four. I had three cards down. It was my turn for the final bet. "Men," I announced glibly, "I'm feeling bad about taking all of your money. I know it's money you need for dating, food, life's other essentials. So, out of the goodness of my heart, I'm giving it all back—that is if you've got the guts." They stared at me in awe. I continued, "I'm feeling lucky—very lucky—so I'm betting my entire pot, all the winnings of the evening on this one hand." I pushed the pile of money sitting before me to the center of the table.

"What are you doin', Harry?" Jason Hanson asked.

"I told you, I feel lucky. I'm betting it all."

"We have a betting limit, you can't do it."

"I'm not asking you to match my bet, just the ten-dollar limit—can't be a rule about that, can there?" They looked dumbfounded.

"Wait a second. You're saying that you're going to bet three hundred bucks or more, while we only have to match the betting limit?"

"Amazing, but true. It's out of the goodness of my heart, you understand," I replied.

Jason jumped first. "I'm in, man, here's my ten." He looked at his last card and dropped his money in the center. He looked confident, showing two pair, fives and threes; jack high. Harvey Langer was next. He scrounged his last ten bucks in dollars and change and placed it on top. He tried to look confident; I guessed he was bluffing. He showed two fours, a two, and a seven. Next, it was Bud's turn. He had the best hand showing; his problem was that he was out of money. He looked around the table suspiciously at them and then at me.

"You guys know I'm tapped out. What do you want?

Hell, I'm already making your bed, Harry, until what? October?"

Jason chimed in, *"It's Harry who's betting the whole wad, I guess he gets to decide what's fair. Harry?"*

Their eyes shifted to me. I tried to act nonchalant. "I don't know. Let's see, there's an awful lot on the table here, I count three hundred sixty bucks, not to mention the bed making, and bathroom cleaning, you're already committed to doing. Yep, there's an awful lot on the table, all right. It'd have to be something worth a lot to give you a chance at winning all this money back."

"Enough dramatics, Harry, what do you want?"

"Here's a thought. That girl you met, what was her name, Kiley, or Catrina?"

"It's Kathryn, Harry, what about her?"

"That's right, Kathryn, I remember now. I'm not doing anything on Friday. I need a date—just for some company, nothing serious. I was thinking that she'd be interesting to talk to, being from Oklahoma and all."

"She's from Texas, Harry, and you're saying you want me to bet my date with Kathryn for Friday night? You're nuts!"

"I'm nuts? You win that pot, Bud, and you'll be eating steak and lobster Friday night with Kelly."

"It's Kathryn."

"Why, you could probably rent a limo and have money left over. Think about it, Bud. If you're not in, you're tapped. You'll be buying her burgers and fries, if you can scrape up that much change. It's all or nothing. Your call. In or not?"

I tried to act as if it was no big deal. Inside, I wanted to die.

"I'm just not sure—I mean, betting my date?"

I reached out my hand and began to fluff the pile of ones, fives, and tens that lay on the table in front of me.

"As I said, Bud, it's your call. Sirloin steaks or greasy burgers—you decide."

He picked up his last card and studied his hand. He had three nines showing, a king, and a ten. If he had the other nine, I would lose. He seemed to smile.

"Okay, I'm in."

Those were the words I had longed to hear.

"No more betting at this point, gentlemen, it's all on the table. Somebody's going to walk away a winner, the rest losers. That's the way the game works. It's a man's game. Win or lose, it's been a helluva ride. What do you say, for the sake of dramatics, we all lay 'em down at the same time?" It was deathly quiet as everyone readied their cards.

Emily, people have defining moments in their lives. Moments when they feel their lives change forever. For some it's the birth of their first child. For others, the night of their first kiss, or getting that promotion at the office. I know it sounds strange, but mine was winning Kathryn that Wednesday night in the game hall at USC. It was a moment etched into my brain that I'll remember until the day I die. I was triumphant.

Of course, after the hoopla had settled down, Bud and I had one small problem to figure out. I'd won Kathryn fair and square, but we couldn't just walk up and tell her. Women are funny about stuff like that. Instead we crafted a plan.

Bud was hesitant, but he had no choice. We decided I would go as the driver—it would be cute—she'd love it. Unfortunately, poor Bud was going to get deathly sick and have to be taken home. Not wanting to ruin the evening for

Kathryn, he would insist in his misery that I take her back to the dance and then on to their dinner reservations. It was ingenious.

For the plan to be realistic, we needed a car worthy of a driver. That was not as easy as it sounds. Typically a limousine is rented with a driver by the hour. To drive it ourselves required a twenty-four hour rental. It cost me a fortune, but it was for Kathryn, so it was cheap. We picked up the car at noon and then spent the rest of the afternoon cruising around town. (We were certainly going to get our money's worth.) At five, we picked up our tuxedos and headed back to the dorm to shower. While Bud's tux was long and formal, mine had a plain black jacket, suitable for the part.

At seven o'clock we reached Kathryn's apartment exactly as planned. Bud took the corsage and walked up to the porch. She was stunning. As they approached the car, I jumped out and swept open the door.

"Ma'am, your car."

"Kathryn, this is Harry, my roommate. Remember, I introduced you after his practice the other day."

"Sure. Hi, Harry." I nodded politely as she stepped inside. Bud glared.

"Harry, to what do we owe the pleasure of you driving us tonight?" she inquired. I had my story all worked out. I certainly couldn't lie to the girl.

"Let's just say that we had a wild game of poker the other night and leave it at that." Bud coughed—no, it was more of a choke.

Her voice was sweet. "You bet stuff like that in poker? Men!" she pronounced with disgust. You have no idea, gorgeous, I thought to myself.

I entered the dance and hung near the back until the

music started. Out of the goodness of my heart, I had agreed to let Bud dance once with her before the illness would hit. I smiled as the band started the evening with a fast dance. Bud looked tense. As the music ended I moved toward the bathroom door and waited. The next dance started and to my horror, Bud continued dancing with my date. He looked nervously toward our meeting spot and when his eyes met mine, I made a quick cutting motion with my hand across my neck. It was fair and square, he was not going to cheat me now.

As the dance ended, he excused himself and headed toward the rest room. I followed him inside.

"What the hell you doing, Bud? It's poker. It's sacred!"

"Harry, I just can't. Let's work something out. I just can't do it. I'm sorry." He had touched an angel, but it was not meant to be.

"One way or another, Bud, trust me when I tell you, you will get sick." I had suspected this might occur and I was ready. "Isn't that right, Jason?" As I spoke, Jason Hanson stepped out from a stall.

"Harry's right. I was there. Saw it with my own eyes. You have to pay up, Bud." Reaching out, Jason grabbed one side, while I grabbed the other. We carried Bud into the closest stall and forced him to bend over. As Jason shoved his face near the water, I flushed.

"Okay, okay. I'll do it. Let me up."

Forcing him next over to the sink, I messed up his tie, while Jason splashed water on the front of his pressed tux.

"Take it easy," he protested, "it's an expensive tux."

"That should do it. Now go out and tell the sweet thing just how sick you've been."

With that, we pushed him out the door and waited. It didn't take long.

"*Glad to have you back, Bud. You're here to vomit again, I presume?*"

The plan was working perfectly, except for one small problem. When we were holding Bud's head in the toilet, we didn't realize another stall was occupied. We didn't hear the door open, or the footsteps of the spy who silently slipped out and ratted on our plan. (It wasn't until years later, Emily, I found out the snitch was whiny Arnold Swenson, the kid I'd beat out for pitching position on the baseball team.)

As we prepared Bud to give the sad news to Kathryn, the door burst open. We looked up from the sink to see Kathryn entering the men's bathroom.

"*Harry?*" We were standing in the far corner and as she entered, two guys standing in front of the urinals quickly zipped up their pants and walked out. She marched right up to where Bud, Jason, and I were standing. I stood in shock. Jason spoke first.

"*You can't just come in here. This is the men's bathroom!*" She glared at him as if to say, *you just try to stop me, pal.*

She spoke defiantly. "*I've got six brothers, honey—it's nothing I haven't seen before, trust me on that one.*" Then she turned to Bud. "*You look like you're feeling much better.*"

He stammered, not sure how to answer. "*Uh, I am, much better.*"

"*I'm so glad to hear that.*" Her tone was sarcastic. "*Gentlemen, what's this talk about me being lost or won in a game of poker?*" I would have expected her to be furious. Instead she was eerily calm. I'm not sure if it was his guilt or Kathryn's alluring Texas accent, but Bud broke down first.

"*I'm so sorry, it was Harry's idea. There was three-hundred and sixty dollars in the pot. I was out of money, and*

Harry said—" Traitor, I thought to myself. She turned to look me square in the eyes.

"Harry? Is this some sort of local tradition, betting your women in poker?" She remained calm but firm. Deep down, I think she was flattered.

"Well, no, ma'am. It's the first time I've ever heard of such a thing." Then stupidly I added, "But it was all fair and square."

"I see. What'd you win with, Harry?"

"I beg your pardon?" I replied.

"Are your ears all clogged up? I said what'd you win me with—what hand?"

"Uh—it was jacks and sixes."

"Jacks and sixes? You won me with jacks and sixes?" She seemed astonished.

"Well, yes, ma'am."

She paused, deep in thought before she spoke. "It seems to me, boys, that if you're going to be betting a woman in a game of poker, as if she were some prize pig to be won at the fair, she ought to at least have a chance to defend herself."

"What are you saying?" Jason questioned. She ignored him, turning to address Bud.

"You got any cards around here?"

"Sure," he replied. "There's a deck in the locker room."

She looked me square in the eyes and challenged—no, it was more than that—she directed, "Come on, Harry, we've got some poker to play."

While Bud ran to get the cards, I followed her like a sheep to a vacant table over behind the refreshment stand. She looked so confident and self-assured. On the way over I tried to make small talk. "You play poker? Not many women I know play poker."

"I told you, Harry, I grew up with six brothers. I was the only girl. I can do a lot more than play poker." I had the sick feeling I was being hustled. "So what's your game, Harry?"

"We usually play seven-card stud, no jokers, ten-dollar limit—but I didn't bring much extra money with me." It was hard to tell but I thought I saw her smile.

"Don't worry, Harry. We won't be playing for money."

She pulled the short train of her gown to one side, and then lifted her skirt just enough to sit comfortably across from me at the table. She pulled off each of her satin gloves and tossed them across the table onto a vacant chair beside me. It was a challenge. I tried to appear confident. Her stare was piercing. Bud arrived with the cards and started to hand them to me but Kathryn reached out, took the deck, and began to shuffle. It was a thing of beauty to behold. Her dress pulled to the side, her hair shining in the dim light, a band playing in the background, and Kathryn handling a deck of cards as if she were kneading bread dough in the kitchen.

In just seconds, she'd shuffled and cut the cards. "Let's play," she announced. "Oh, and since we're not playing for money, how about we play five-card draw, no wilds, three-draw maximum?"

"Sure, sounds great."

No sooner had I agreed than cards were lying before me on the table.

She looked me in the eyes as she spoke. "Here's the deal, Harry." There was no question, she was in charge. "You said you won me fair and square, but that isn't so because I wasn't there. You want to play for the right to take me home, then fine. If you win this hand, you get to take me home tonight from the dance."

"And if I lose?"

"*If you lose,*" she looked around the room, "*if you lose, you walk over to that punch bowl and kiss the bottom of it,*" then she added, "*from the inside.*"

"*You're saying I have to dunk my head in the punch bowl?*"

"*You are such a smart boy.*"

I had no choice. If I had even the slightest chance of taking this incredible, poker-playing creature home, I'd have walked to the end of the earth.

"*Let's do it,*" I answered, picking up my cards. I'd been dealt a good hand. I had two pair, eights and fours, jack high. I tried to look calm. She stared into my eyes. My decision was an easy one. I tossed in the jack and tried for a full house; that would seal my win for sure.

"*I'll take one,*" I responded, slinging my card toward her slender fingers.

"*And I'll take two,*" she spoke almost to herself as she dealt our cards.

My heart raced as I peeked at my card. Nothing that would help; I'd have to win with two pair.

"*Harry, do you want to up the ante, or call?*" My hand was good, but she seemed so sure of herself.

"*I think we should just read 'em and weep.*"

"*If you say so,*" she consented. "*What have you got?*" As I revealed my hand, a murmur arose from the small crowd that had gathered to watch. She laid her cards down and revealed a pair of queens and a pair of nines, king high.

My heart sank. "*Sorry, Harry. I hope you like punch.*"

As I was about to stand and take my punishment, she continued, "*Of course, we could go one more hand if you'd like, perhaps for some bigger stakes.*"

"*What do you mean?*"

"We'll play one more. If you win, you'll still get to take me home. But if I win—" she turned to Bud, who actually appeared to be enjoying the show, "Bud, are there still chickens up in the biology lab?"

"Sure, I saw them today in class."

"Okay then, if you lose, Harry, you'll get a chicken from the biology lab, take it to the middle of the dance floor, and in front of all these people, you'll kiss its beak for a full minute."

"What? You want me to kiss a chicken?"

"Yep, those are the stakes. This is a man's game. Are you man enough?" Her words sounded familiar. It was strange, everyone was there with dates, but as the game continued, the women seemed to separate from the men, gathering behind Kathryn's side of the table; the men moved to stand behind mine. I wasn't just playing to win Kathryn, I was representing my gender. I could feel the pressure building.

It's hard to know what to do, Emily, in these situations. I was being hustled, big time, but what were my choices? I could dunk my head in the punch or take another chance for Kathryn.

"I'll tell you what," I replied, "if I lose, I'll kiss the chicken. In fact, I'll kiss the chicken for a full minute and then I'll dunk my head in the punch bowl, and then I'll stick my face in that cake over there on the table. But if I win, I not only get to drive you home, I get to take you out onto the dance floor and kiss you for a full minute." The men's hoots filled the room.

She seemed intrigued, but never flinched.

"You're on. Your turn to deal." She pushed the deck of cards in my direction, but I politely refused.

"You go ahead and deal," I directed, "I don't want to be accused of cheating when I win." I wasn't trying to be a gentleman. I knew that my card-shuffling abilities would dim in comparison to hers. Within what seemed like seconds, she'd shuffled and had our cards dealt in perfect piles on the table.

I picked up my hand. The poker gods were not kind. The crowd of men behind me groaned when I asked for three cards. She took one. We laid down our cards and again the women's side of the table cheered as I lost once more—this time to a lousy pair of jacks.

"You've hit a cold streak, Harry. Perhaps, you ought to be a tad more careful about what you're betting when you play this game."

I was humiliated. She had me kissing a chicken, dunking my head in punch, and then plowing my face into a cake. Instead of watching me suffer, she surprised me.

"Let's go one more," she suggested.

I'd already lost my dignity, not to mention Kathryn. What else mattered?

"Sure. Now what?" I asked, leaving my fate in her hands.

"Same stakes as before, but if you lose, you also climb to the top of the diving tower down by the pool, you strip stark-naked, and jump off while yelling, 'men are morons.'" The women watching roared at the prospect.

"You want me to strip naked?" I quizzed.

"There's that strange echo, again," she added, as the giggles subsided.

"Deal," I answered coldly.

She whipped the cards onto the table. I showed three kings, a six, and a ten. Respectable. I tried to read her eyes. They were beautiful, but showed no hint of the hand she held.

"I'll take two." I tried to sound distraught. She dealt two cards to the table and watched as I picked them up. I wanted *to jump up and down with joy. I'd drawn two threes for a full house. I'd be hard to beat. She stared at me while announcing, "And I'll take two." She dealt herself two cards and placed them on the table in front of her. She hadn't even looked at them, when she asked, "What do you have, Harry?"*

"Aren't you going to look at what you drew?"

"Nope, what do you have?"

I threw my hand down for everyone to see. As I did, the men cheered.

"Full house. Nice hand," she responded, "But—" She seemed so calm, so confident. Slowly she dropped her cards onto the table one by one. A queen, another queen, and then the third. The first emotion she showed was a grin as she studied the look on my face. I'm sure she saw sheer terror. A full house would still beat three queens, but her two drawn cards lay menacingly on the table. She pulled up the corner of the first card, all emotion now gone. With a flick of her wrist, she flipped over a seven. Sighs of relief flowed from the men around me. One card left. I knew we hadn't seen the other queen. If she had it, she'd beat me with four-of-a-kind and I'd be the laughing stock of the school for months. If it were any other card, I'd have pulled off the biggest coup of my life. Calmly, she reached out and pulled the card toward her, all the while looking directly into my eyes. She lifted the corner slightly, and glanced down so nobody else could sneak a look. Her expression never changed as she examined her card and then looked back into my eyes. I couldn't look away. It was as if she were pondering which way to go, as if she could somehow will that card to be anything she desired. After what felt like minutes, she stood up and with one single motion, she pushed that card back into the middle of the deck, which lay in the center of the table.

"Looks like Harry here beat me!" she announced to the crowd. The holler from the men's side erupted as the women sighed and started to filter away. Kathryn didn't flinch but kept her eyes locked on mine. I reached out to take her hand, and we walked together to the middle of the floor. As the band played and couples began to dance once more, I collected my winnings with what was the most romantic one-minute kiss of my entire life.

We were inseparable afterwards and married seven months later. To this day, Emily, I still don't know what card she drew.

I do, however, have one confession I need to make. It's something that has haunted me my entire life. I told you I'd won the first game fair and square, the game in the men's hall that Wednesday. I'd be a liar if I didn't confess the game was rigged. I paid my entire winnings that night, short of the date with Kathryn, to Jason Hanson, who slipped me his cards for that final hand.

I was wrong, Emily. Even for Kathryn, I should not have cheated. I was young and foolish and I thought it was the only way to win her without ruining my friendship with Bud. I went about it the wrong way. I did finally confess to Bud, a few years later. He made me pay him three hundred and sixty bucks with interest, plus take him and his wife out to dinner. We laughed about it for hours. It was still wrong.

The question then, granddaughter, is what lesson does this teach? I would hope you'd forget the cheating part and simply remember how much I loved your grandmother. My life changed forever the day she came into it.

You'll know, Emily, when you meet the right person as well. And when you know, grab on with both arms and never let go. Oh, you'll have troubles, Kathryn and I did, but we never stopped loving each other. We waited seven months to get married because of her mother—she wanted us to be sure. In our case it wouldn't have mattered, but it's good advice. Do the same for me, Emily. It seems prudent.

I'll be watching you.

Love,

Grandpa Harry

Emily scampered into the kitchen still in her pajamas and caught Laura crying. It was a scene she was getting accustomed to seeing. Laura motioned her over.

"Come here, babe, I want to read you a story about how your grandpa and grandma met."

Emily listened intently as Laura read the letter aloud.

"That's way cool, Mom."

Laura couldn't help but smile. "Should we call your dad and tell him the secret?"

"Sure. I'll dial." Emily picked up the phone and dialed Bob's number.

The letter was a gem. Laura had known nothing about Emily's grandmother Kathryn. She wasn't sure Bob knew much about her either, as he'd been just a child when she died.

"Daddy, it's me."

"Good morning, honey, how are you?"

"Fine. Mommy has a secret to tell you—just a second." She passed the phone to Laura.

"Hi."

"Well?" he questioned.

"They were real people, Bob. She was vibrant and funny and impetuous—and they were so in love."

"What?"

"Do you have any idea how your mom and dad met?"

"No. I don't."

"I do and it's amazing. We got so used to him as an old man, we forgot he was once like us. Do you want to hear the story? And your mother was incredible!"

"Okay, I'm interested. Tell me."

"It's the fourth poem. Read it slowly. Then draw a circle around their names. Connect the circles with a straight line and you'll see the password."

"Oh, come on, Laura, just tell me."

"I want you to see it on your own. Read me the phrase and I'll fax you his letter. I'd read it to you but it's several pages long. Believe me, it's beautiful."

She waited patiently while he retrieved the book and looked up the poem. "Love at first sight," he replied. "He tells her to believe in it. Hey, that's kind of tricky the way he did that."

"Close enough. It's an amazing story, Bob. Here it comes."

"Wait," he interrupted, "before you hang up, is there any way to copy the files and send them to me on a disk? That way we won't have to keep calling at all hours?" The truth was Laura was beginning to enjoy the calls. "Oh, I talked to Michelle as well. She wants to know if you can send her the last book and a copy of the files as well. She about freaked when I told her what we found. She's pretty good at puzzles—I figure the more help, the better."

"No problem. I already have Michelle's book packed. I'll copy the files and run to the mail center right now."

"Laura? Thanks."

As the fax machine sucked the printed pages through, she opened up the phone book and scanned the names for the number of Dr. Steve Iverly.

CHAPTER *Thirteen*

$\mathcal{S}$HE SAT ON HOLD FOR ALMOST FIFTEEN MINUTES BEFORE he picked up. She'd insisted to the receptionist that it was a medical emergency.

"Good morning. This is Dr. Iverly. Sorry to make you wait."

"Hi, this is Laura Whitney. Remember me?"

"Now that's a foolish question. Certainly, Laura. Is there a problem?"

She was embarrassed. "It's not actually an emergency. It was the only way I knew I could get through. Of course if it were an emergency, I'd be dead by now."

She could not see the doctor smile. "Whatever it takes, I guess. So, Laura, how can I help?"

"I know you said you weren't a specialist, but I really don't know who else to call. Can I just ask you a couple more questions?"

"About—let's see—it was Harry, right?"

"Yes."

"I'll help if I can."

"I found a prescription for norepinephrine. Can you tell me what it's generally prescribed for?"

"It helps to stabilize a chemical imbalance—specifically, it controls chemical production in the brain."

"Does that mean it's a depression medication?"

"Essentially, yes."

"What would happen if someone were taking this and then their prescription ran out or they forgot to take it? Would it be noticeable?"

"Sure, especially if it were successful in treating the condition."

"That's just what Dr. Jensen said."

"Dr. Jensen? So, I'm your second opinion?"

"No, you were my first, remember? He was the second opinion. Now you're—well, you're the second opinion on the second opinion." He laughed. "Listen," Laura continued, "I hope you don't think I'm crazy, but I think you were right in your guess about Harry."

"What do you mean?"

"I think there was more going on than just Alzheimer's. There were times—a few minutes, even hours, each day—when he was coherent. Other times he seemed distant, confused, angry—like a different person. I've been reading about the disease and from what I read, if AD had taken his life he would have been close to helpless. He wasn't."

"Okay, then what do you think he had?"

"You were the one who first suggested mental illness. It just fits. Harry had all the symptoms of depression, quite a few of which could have been mistaken for signs of AD. And he was on a prescription of norepinephrine. Don't get me wrong; I think Harry probably was in the early stages of Alzheimer's— there were certainly signs of it. But more than that, I think he was suffering from depression. And I think he probably had it for most of his life. Does my theory make sense?"

"When do you start medical school?"

"So, you think it's valid?"

"From everything you've told me, I think you could very well have nailed it on the head."

She wanted to reach through the phone and kiss him. "Can I ask you one last thing?"

"Talk all day." He couldn't see her blush.

"Harry's wife died at a very early age. Would that have caused the depression?"

"I wish you'd call an expert in the mental health field."

"Right now, you are my expert."

"I wouldn't say it caused it as there's a hereditary component involved, but it certainly could have triggered it."

"So, you're saying if Harry had some form of depression, perhaps his father or mother had it as well?"

"Or someone else perched up in the family tree. In fact, it's not only possible, statistically it's probable. Remember, mental illness affects more than twenty million adults. It's the most common brain disease in the country."

"Twenty million?"

"That's what studies show. Some people live with it, have a normal life; others get bad enough they need professional help, even medication. Sadly enough, some end up living on the street. Whether moderate or severe, depression is nothing to be ashamed of or scared about."

"I want you to know, Doctor . . ."

"Please, call me Steve."

"Steve, I want you to know that I deeply appreciate your help. You're a very kind person, and that's rare these days."

"I appreciate the compliment, but it isn't necessary and it's not rare. Just look around."

Laura paused, contemplating his words. "You're right. I don't mean to be negative. It's not rare at all, is it?"

"No, not at all." He hesitated before continuing. "Laura, do you mind if I ask you a personal question?"

"No, what?"

"If Emily is your daughter, should I presume that you're married?"

She was flattered at his inquiry but didn't hesitate in her response. "I am."

"Figured so. The cute ones always are."

"Thanks, Steve."

"You're welcome, anytime. Take care."

She arrived late to the sales meeting at the office. Because he knew she was having problems with her marriage, Grant Midgley didn't ask for an excuse. The office was swamped. She was given her share of callbacks generated at the model home over the weekend, and except for a meeting she had with a client at noon, she spent the day on the phone.

By the time she finished returning her last call, she was sure the phone had been attached to her ear. It was just about time to head home if she was to get there before Emily arrived. While she gathered up her things, the phone rang again. It was Bob.

"You know how I always liked riddles? This thing is addictive."

"I just have a second. I have to get home before Emily."

"Sorry. I'll be quick. I don't know if these are supposed to be read in any order, but take a look at poem sixteen. It says, find a jewel and win the prize."

"Okay, so?"

"Well, two lines down it says 'I am proud I am on display for all to see.' "

She didn't have the book with her, but jotted down the words as Bob recited them. "Keep going."

"Did you write the words down?"

"I did."

"Well, underline the *d* in *proud* and then the *d* in the word *display*."

"Okay."

"Do you see it yet?"

"Bob, if I don't hurry, I'll miss Emily's bus."

"Sorry. Now underline all the letters in between and read me the name of the jewel we need to win the prize."

She smiled. "Diamond."

"Try it and call me when you get home. Also, number twelve—I know you're in a hurry so I won't torture you. The password's 'Angel.' " Her laptop was in her briefcase. She'd try them when she got home. "Did you send the disk?" he continued.

"I sent it overnight. You should get it today. Call me if you don't."

"Okay. One more quick item. I just talked to Greg. You know, my sister sure married a creep."

"What's up?"

"Greg thinks we should contest the will. Says it's not right for Emily to get the house, while they just get a few thousand dollars."

"What did you tell him?"

"Nothing yet. I told him I'd get back to him. I mean I can

certainly see his point, but at the same time, it was Harry's money. Isn't it his right to give it to whomever he pleases? My attorney says the will is probably valid. It depends on when it was written and when the symptoms of Alzheimer's started to set in—you know, if he was of '*sound mind*' or not. What do you think I should tell Greg?"

"I'm not sure. I don't mean to cut you short, but Emily will be locked out if I don't run now. Can I call you later to discuss this?"

"Sure, sorry. Bye."

She wasn't sure if Bob hung up mad or not. Sometimes it was hard to tell.

Traffic was light. She arrived home with six minutes to spare. While she waited for Emily, she turned on the computer and opened the sixteenth letter. It looked like Bob was right. "Clever, Harry. Very clever." She leaned back in the chair, made herself comfortable and began to read.

Dearest Emily,

People will tell you that if you leave wasps alone, they will leave you alone. Poppycock! Those people have never spent much time in a garden. I have been stung countless times when I was just minding my own business. Did it keep me from enjoying my garden? Only once. It dawns on me, Emily, that a wasp sting teaches an important lesson in life. Let me explain.

One day while working in my garden, a wasp landed on my shoulder. When I tried to brush him aside, I flicked him onto my neck where he promptly stung me. I'd been stung before, but this was one sting too many. Angry, I went to the shed and I grabbed a can of spray and a fly swatter. I covered my face with cheesecloth and put on a hat to cover my bald head. I pulled on a thick, long-sleeved shirt and snatched a pair of gloves. I was headed to the garden for a war. My mission was to eliminate any wasp that buzzed within fifty yards of my garden.

Two hours later, the potatoes were still full of weeds that hadn't been hoed, the water hadn't been turned on, and I hadn't fertilized the carrots. It didn't matter, I was going to kill all the wasps God ever created; and I had done a great job. I had killed dozens of them. The problem was that they never seemed to go away. I'm sure I looked ridiculous, waving and swatting and spraying and jumping around. It took me half a day to realize how crazy I was being. There would always be more wasps than I could kill, and I was miserable.

Life is the same. There will be times when you are minding your own business, hurting no one. Then someone will come along and sting you. You have two choices. One is to get angry and waste days of your life swatting at anyone who looks threatening; if you do, you'll find when you're through, you've accomplished nothing. The better path is to protect yourself the best you can, and then enjoy your garden. When you get stung, it will hurt; you may cry and wonder what you have done to deserve such treatment. Let it end there. Take a deep breath, place a dab of wet mud on the sting, wipe your tears, and put a smile back on your face. Turn back to your garden and enjoy the beauty before you. I hope this makes sense. Now, go tend to your garden and enjoy it immensely.

Love,
Grandpa Harry

Laura printed a copy and then clicked on number twelve. She typed in "Angel" and watched the file open. She was about to start reading when Emily scurried through the door.

"Hi, honey."

"Hey, Mom."

"Do you have papers to show me today?"

"Yeah. Are there any more letters from Grandpa?"

"Yes, actually two more today."

"Can we read them?"

"Sure, I was just about to start one. Let's read it together; then you can show me your stuff."

Laura printed the letter and then plopped down next to Emily on the couch.

Dearest Emily,

You need to be aware as you grow into an adult that you are an angel. These words are not meant as a trivial compliment of affection from a grandfather to his grand-daughter. I mean literally, you are an "angel." Let me explain.

I don't remember if I ever told you but your grand-mother, Kathryn, was a seamstress. She had majored in Clothing and Textiles and was very skilled in creating beautiful dresses. When we were first married, she began to specialize in sewing wedding gowns and very quickly had more work than she could handle. I convinced her to raise her prices, which she did, but even so the demand often exceeded her time. She quickly gained a tremendous reputation in the area as a skilled couturier. One day she had an appointment to meet a girl at St. James Cathedral over in East Milford. In front of the church there is a beautiful fountain, which Kathryn had always admired. She finished her appointment early and with time to spare, she decided to sit by the fountain and sketch out several designs for her client. While she enjoyed the splendor of the morning, she struck up a conversation with a girl who had also come to admire the fountain's beauty. Her name was Andrea. Kathryn was always an easy person to talk with and so in their conversation, she learned that Andrea had come from a small town in Oklahoma. As with Kathryn's earlier appointment, she was also to be married in the church— just not under as favorable circumstances. She had become pregnant and as such had been disowned by her parents. She and the boy had moved into his aunt's basement nearby and were planning to get married on their own in the coming weeks. When Kathryn asked what she planned to wear, Andrea admitted she had nothing, as she worried about any dress fitting in her condition.

Right then and there, Kathryn offered to make her a dress at no charge. Told her some story about being a new seamstress who needed to learn how to fit a dress to someone expecting. She told Andrea she'd even be doing her a favor to let her "practice." That's the type of person Kathryn was. I had watched Kathryn sew many a wedding gown, but this particular gown she seemed to enjoy just a bit more.

The day of the wedding came and the dress Kathryn created was stunning. Later in the day, after the ceremony, Andrea pulled Kathryn aside and through her tears she called Kathryn her "angel." She explained how weeks before, at the fountain, she had been an emotional wreck, frustrated and confused about her situation and condition. She said she had just thrown a few coins into the fountain, closed her eyes, and wished for an angel; seconds later, Kathryn had sat down beside her. My point, Emily, is that to Andrea, Kathryn was indeed an angel. She came and helped out in a time of need.

To some it may seem meaningless. It was, after all, only a dress. To Andrea, it was the world. It is the same with all of us. If we will but look around, we can be actual angels to those around us in need.

Be sensitive, my dear granddaughter. Be caring, and you too can be an angel as well.

Love,

Grandpa Harry

Laura watched Emily. She didn't say a word, and it looked like she might be crying. Gets it from me, no doubt, Laura thought, giving Emily a squeeze.

"Do you understand what Grandpa is telling you?"

She nodded. Laura knew the letters would become even more meaningful as Emily grew older—when she could understand them better.

"Mom, do you think Grandma was pretty?"

"I'm sure she was very pretty."

"Do you remember her?"

"Well, no, sweetie. She died when your daddy was just little—younger than you, I guess. But if she looked like you, she must have been beautiful." Emily looked pensive. "But that's the most wonderful part of these letters," Laura continued. "Grandpa's telling us all about her—so we'll know her. She was a very special person, just like you."

"I miss her, Mom, though I never knew her."

"I didn't know her either, but I miss her as well."

"Let's read the other one, and then we'll fax these to Dad."

When they had finished, she dialed Bob's number and waited for him to pick up.

"Hi, this is Bob Whitney. I'm not in, so please leave a message at the tone or press two to send a fax."

She dropped the sheets into the fax machine and pressed the button. She felt bad about having cut him off so quickly earlier in the day. She'd try him later after Emily was in bed. That way they could talk freely about Greg and what to do with the will.

CHAPTER *Fourteen*

MICHELLE WAS THRILLED TO FIND THE PACKAGE SITTING by the door. She had been on pins and needles since Bob had first told her about the book.

It was larger than she had expected. Fascinating. She opened the volume carefully. Stunning fabric, she thought, as she examined its construction. The cover was stitched around the edges by hand with a thick cord and then tied on each inside face with a bow. The book was thick and sturdy. She had an hour before the kids would arrive home, so she sat down and began to read.

Many of the words felt familiar and reminded her of her childhood home. Bob seemed to hold such bitter memories of home. She remembered it more fondly. It wasn't paradise, but lots of kids had worse, she decided. It would have been nice, though, to have had a mother around the house;

it would have helped Bob. It was funny how she still worried about him. It was so difficult living far away. In their phone conversations, Bob never seemed happy, always discontent. In many ways he reminded her of Harry, though in a million years, she'd never tell him so.

Her hands touched the cover lightly. She flipped cautiously from page to page, glancing at the words. So, Dad had written poems—poems with messages. It was intriguing. She turned back to those Bob and Laura had already solved. Sure enough, she could see the passwords. Of course it was easy, if you already knew the answers.

She moved on to some of the riddles that hadn't yet been solved and began to read—read and think about home.

Bob seemed almost frantic when Laura answered the phone.

"Are you sitting down?"

"No, do I need to be?"

"You're not going to believe this."

"What? Which one did you solve?"

"No more yet."

"What then?"

"Well, it was Greg—er, rather his kids—actually I'm not sure how it happened. They were playing with the book and . . ."

"Playing with it? Why were they playing with it?"

"I don't know, just get the book, sit down, and listen." Laura grabbed the book from the table, switched to the cordless phone, and sat on the couch without saying a word. Emily was playing in her room.

After a few seconds, Bob spoke.

"You there?"

"I'm here. You told me to sit down and listen."

"Sorry. Now open the back cover."

She did as instructed. "Okay, the back cover is open."

"Untie the string."

"Huh?"

"The string that's stitched around the cover and then tied with a bow on the inside. Untie the bow on the back cover and lift up the flap. When you do, the middle section of the cover will slide out. Do it and tell me what you find."

Laura pulled on the string and indeed it held down a flap folded underneath. Three thin boards sandwiched together were used to make the cover. When she pulled the center sheet out, a gold coin hidden in a round cutout dropped to the floor. She picked it up off the carpet and examined it.

"Bob?"

"Wait, don't tell me. I bet it's a 1908 Saint-Gaudens gold piece—in almost mint condition. How am I doing?"

"But, how?"

"From what I gather, they found it by accident. My guess is that one of Harry's poems or letters tells us it's there, we just don't know which one yet. Greg thinks it's the gold poem, but I'm not so sure. Can you believe he hid gold in the book?"

"Your dad is certainly full of surprises."

"It gets more bizarre. Greg freaked out. He thinks there might be more gold in the house so 'Mr. only has time to visit at Christmas' has arranged a few days off so he and Michelle can come out and check."

"There're coming out here?"

"Sure enough. They'll be there Wednesday. Here's the funny part—Greg wondered if any gold coins we find at the house would be classified as savings, as described in Harry's will. One minute he wants to contest it, saying Harry was not of right mind, now he's ready to make Harry a saint. Can you believe him?"

"Do you think there's any more gold? We went through the house pretty thoroughly, didn't we?"

"Who knows what's hidden there. With all these secret poems, passwords, and now gold coins, you must admit, it makes you wonder. After all, the color always intrigued him. If you stood next to Harry for ten minutes, he'd paint you gold. With the hidden gold coins showing up, I'm not sure what to think anymore. Either way, though, I'll be coming out to meet Greg and Michelle. I've already made the arrangements. I don't want Greg tearing up the place without someone there to watch him. I thought I'd let you know."

"Thanks, Bob."

"Sure. See you in a couple of days."

Laura placed the coin back into the binding and tied the cover back together. As she did, she spoke softly to herself. "What are you up to now, Harry?"

She arrived at the clinic wearing a white ball gown, the one that had been stored in the basement. She looked stunning, and as the elevator doors opened, the gown's layers oozed from the opening. She waltzed proudly to the reception desk.

"I'm here to see Dr. Steve Iverly," she announced loudly, so everyone waiting in the room was sure to hear.

"Do you have your patient number?" the gray-haired lady inquired coldly. Laura reached for her purse. It was completely empty. She had left the number he had given her sitting on the floor at home.

"I don't have it, but he's waiting to see me. He called and

asked me to come." The phone on the receptionist's desk began to ring.

"I'm sorry, ma'am, but without your patient number you're not getting past me."

"You have to let me in, he's waiting. He wants me to go with him. He just called." The phone continued its incessant ring.

"That's him trying to call. Aren't you going to answer it?"

"No, ma'am. I'm not the operator, just the receptionist. The operator won't be back until Tuesday." *Ring, ring, ring.* Laura was getting hysterical.

"It's him and he needs me to go with him. I have his tuxedo right here—see it's his size—he's waiting for me. You must answer the phone." *Ring, ring, ring.*

"No, ma'am. Not until Tuesday." *Ring, ring, ring.*

The phone jarred her awake from the dream as it continued to ring. It took two more rings before she could find it on the nightstand and pick it up.

"Hello?" she muttered.

"I found another one."

"What?"

"Man, it feels good to be the one waking you up. You heard me, I found another one. Turn to page thirteen and read the poem."

She knew Bob had been fascinated with the hidden passwords and Harry's letters, but this was ridiculous. He was, however, being civil so she hated to complain. "Okay, just a second. Let me get it." She climbed out of bed, searched for her robe in the darkness, and then tiptoed down the stairs. The book was still on the table from the night before. She flipped it open to poem eight, headed to the computer, and began to read.

Grandma's Family Portrait

Forty-one had gathered for their portrait shot with pride;
They were all extended family, who had come from far and wide.
Jim and Jill from Tallahassee, Fred and June from River-cress;
Uncle Mike and his young wife, who wore a very low-cut dress.

Linda Ann and Uncle Henry, he's the one who likes to hunt;
And Grandma, ninety-three now, who was sitting right in front.
They had gathered here for Grandma, looking proper, prim, and priss;
It should be a nice occasion, yet something seemed amiss.

Oh, Grandma isn't smiling, noticed crazy Uncle Clyde;
It's cause Grandpa's gone, said Wilma, she's been sad now since he died.
Let's all help, she must be happy, something funny we must do;
She'll be smiling in the picture, if it's up to me and you!

Sandy pulled a silly face, as big Johnny waltzed a dance;
Cousin Kenny told a joke, and old Henry dropped his pants.
They all giggled 'cept for Grandma, who reached up to wipe her
    eye;
So little Amy tugged her sleeve, "Dear Grandma, don't you cry."

She raised her hand to wipe a tear? No, something else instead;
She held her hand across her mouth and this is what she said,
"I'm not sad, the old coot's dead and gone, it is not quite what you
    think;
The reason I'm not smiling is—I left my dentures in the sink."

    Laura had read the poem several times and it still made her chuckle. "Okay, where is it?" she questioned.

    "Take the first letter of every stanza and tell me what it spells."

"Let's see—it spells *floss?*"

"Exactly." He sounded triumphant.

"Floss?" she repeated.

"Why not? It's good advice."

Laura turned on her computer, opened the folder, clicked on the eleventh file, and entered the password.

"Well, I'll be, you're right. Way to go, Bob."

"Thanks." He sounded proud of his feat.

"Want me to read it to you? It's only half a page long."

"I read it. I got your disk. I just thought you'd like to see it."

"Really?"

"Yes, really."

"Thanks. Hang on just a second, while I read it." She quickly scanned the letter.

Dearest Emily,

Have you ever seen an eighty-year-old man with his teeth sitting in the bathroom sink? Trust me, it ain't a pretty sight. Flossing takes just a few seconds each evening but the rewards are tremendous. Oh, you'll have nights when you get home late and you think, "I'll just do it in the morning." Don't succumb! Open the drawer, break off a piece of the white, waxy string and floss.

Two wonderful things will happen. First, throughout your life you'll never be afraid to smile. Second, when you're a ninety-year-old grandmother looking at yourself in the mirror, you will see your smile and you will remember me. Take care of yourself, Emily. I love you.

Love,

Grandpa Harry

"When did he write this stuff, Laura? It's weird. He never told me to floss."

"Don't you see? It's not hygiene advice; he wants to be remembered."

"It just doesn't sound like him."

"I think it does. Think back a few years, before he was sick. Remember how witty he used to be? He wasn't always so stubborn."

"Not from what I can recall."

"All you ever saw in him, since I've known you, is an angry old man."

His natural reaction was to argue, to justify his position, but Bob knew she was right. "You and Emily have been visiting him for what, a couple of years now?"

She stopped to calculate. "It'll be just over two next month."

"Did you ever see him writing?"

"Not often, but Cara mentioned it a few times. I think he liked to write in the morning. Remember, he could have been working on these books for years. In fact, he must have been."

"It's just so bizarre. This is supposed to be from my father, but it feels like advice from a stranger."

"Perhaps that's the reason he wrote it. Did you ever consider that?" she replied.

"Guess I better let you go, it's late. Oh, I think I just about have number seventeen worked out. If I get it tonight, I'll call you. If not, I'll have it by the time I get there on Friday for sure."

"I'll look forward to it, but Bob?"

"Yes?"

"In the morning. If you figure it out tonight, call me in the morning." *Click.*

"Laura? Laura?"

CHAPTER *Fifteen*

$\mathscr{A}$S BOB EXITED THE PLANE, HE FLASHED LAURA WHAT looked like a peace sign. He knew she would understand it meant he'd found the passwords to two more poems. As he approached, he seemed unsure how to greet her. A handshake seemed ridiculous, but a hug felt inappropriate as well. He settled on neither, choosing instead to launch into the news of his discovery.

"Two more, Laura. I'm on a roll. I found one of them on the plane on the way over. When I let out a holler, the flight attendant rushed over to see if everything was okay." He looked around the terminal as if someone might be listening and then bent over to whisper in her ear. "And I'm embarrassed to admit it, but I called in sick yesterday. I sat at the kitchen table all day trying to figure out these silly poems."

"Tell me what you found."

"I have the files on my laptop. I'll read you the letters in the car on the way to the hotel."

"Hotel?"

"Yeah, I made hotel arrangements. Should I cancel them?"

"The midnight phone calls will kill me. If you're okay with it, you can sleep in the guest room again."

"Thanks, that'd be great."

While Laura pulled out of the airport parking lot, Bob booted his computer and loaded the files.

"The first one is the chocolate pudding poem."

"You found that one?" Laura was elated. The poem included two chocolate dessert recipes. She'd been working on it herself and found it perplexing.

"Yes, I did, thank you. It took me a while to figure out. I actually made both recipes again last night before I got clued in to where he was going." Laura smiled. She had two pans of the dessert in her refrigerator from the previous night as well. "The key is in the ingredients, Laura. They are listed differently so it throws you off, but if you look carefully you'll see they are the same—both recipes use the exact same ingredients. Here, let me read the letter and you'll understand."

She continued to drive while Bob typed in the password and then began to read.

Dearest Emily,

   Did you ever wonder what the difference is between chocolate soufflé and chocolate pudding? I know the question sounds crazy, but stay with me on this one and you will soon understand.

   In college I took a job at David Angela's, a restaurant in the ritzy part of town. While most of the desserts we served were purchased frozen from a supplier, thawed, and then presented as if fresh, we did actually make our own chocolate soufflé. It was an old family recipe and a house specialty. It was served on a white plate drizzled with raspberry and chocolate syrup. Belgian chocolate was grated on top with just a sprinkle of powdered sugar. It was always made from scratch and it was a sight to behold. While I was there, I actually learned how to prepare it. Can you believe that? Your grandpa in the kitchen cooking. Just the thought scared Kathryn. After we got married, she kicked me out of the kitchen. She said it was 'cause I never cleaned up my mess, but I knew it was because my chocolate soufflé put her to shame.

Anyway, one day I picked up Kathryn, who was getting her hair done—something I've honestly never understood. Why would you ever pay someone to make your hair look funny, so you can't sleep normally for days, afraid you'll mess it up? Strange custom. Anyway, her hair wasn't finished, so while I waited, I scanned several of the magazines on the table. There were no outdoor magazines, so I picked up one about cooking and started to flip through its pages. In my flipping, I came across a recipe for chocolate pudding. Yes, chocolate pudding. Not the instant kind, the homemade kind, but chocolate pudding nonetheless. I stared at the recipe and realized the ingredients were exactly the same as the chocolate soufflé I had made at the restaurant. The only real difference between the two was the time and manner in which the ingredients were put together and the way it was presented.

It dawned on me right then and there, Emily, that life is very much like gourmet cooking. The ingredients we are given are often the same as those that others receive. It is how those *ingredients are put together—the detail, the time, and the presentation—that make the difference. While some make pudding, others take just a bit more time, go to a little extra trouble, present their creations properly, and create something sumptuous.*

So go to the kitchen, Emily, take the ingredients you've been given in life, and make your grandpa a chocolate soufflé.

Love,

Grandpa Harry

"That's the chocolate pudding advice. The one I found on the plane was the 'Safety in Numbers' poem."

"Read it to me again."

"Sure." He picked up Harry's book, flipped to the poem, and began to read.

Find Safety in Numbers

Some may choose to run this race alone, this journey we call life;
They will say you have less baggage, in a world so full of strife.

Now of this, I'm just not certain, if the path is strewn with stones;
And the world is dark and lonely, it seems cold to walk alone.

Where we're going, rooms aplenty, bring a friend, come arm in arm;
It will make the travel pleasant, keep each other far from harm.

And if two is much less lonely, gather ten all hand in hand;
Bring a light to shine for others, keep away from shifting sand.

So when eighty-two and looking back, I hope to hear some say;
I'm here 'cause someone brought me, he helped me find my way.

"This one was tricky," Bob announced. "The clue is in the

title. '*Find*' Safety in '*Numbers*.' I found the numbers in the poem: that would be two, ten and eighty-two. You type them together and it gets you in."

He pulled up the laptop, entered the password, and read the accompanying letter.

Dearest Emily,

A great man once said, "On small hinges turn the gates of our lives." What it means is that little mistakes can often cause such a great loss of joy. I know this all too well. Guard against it. To do this, establish a set of guiding principles in your life and then live by them faithfully. If you do, they will serve as a map, steering you out of dangerous situations and into rewarding ones. Those principles will keep you on the path, avoiding wrong turns of circumstance and pressures of the day. Never compromise your principles, as one small turn can veer you into more difficult paths. Let me illustrate with a story.

Shortly after moving into our home, a friend invited me to go camping. It was a "men only" trip. I believe today they call it "male bonding," or some such ridiculous term. Anyway, he picked up a few maps from the U.S. Geological Survey and we set out to explore the east range up near Diamond Fork. The trails were easy to follow, and in our exploration we discovered a beautiful natural hot spring in Corner Canyon. A waterfall of chilly mountain water cascaded over a granite cliff into a clear pool at the very point where two scalding mineral springs fed into the water. The mix of water temperatures coupled with the crisp morning air caused a strange swirling of steam above the pool, blanketing the area with a mist. It was serene and yet breathtaking. I wanted to share the beauty with Kathryn, so I arranged a weekend when I would take her there. We packed our supplies and headed out, but in my haste I left the map sitting on the counter at home. When we discovered my mistake, Kathryn thought we should return for it. I assured her it wouldn't be necessary; I had been there before and was good at remembering directions. You can guess the outcome, Emily. Without the map, I missed one turn on the trail. That one missed turn caused another and then another. Before I realized where we were, we had hiked miles in the wrong direction. It was dark by the time we retraced our steps to the car, and we never reached the beauty of the crystal pool that day.

So often, Emily, such is life. One wrong turn can catapult us off into the wrong direction. Often before we figure out the mistake and get back on the path, we have missed an opportunity—one that is lost forever.

If you sit down early and decide where you are going in life, and then set some guiding principles to get you there, you will create your very own map. Then, when difficult decisions come or when storm clouds gather, you won't be confused for you will already know which path will lead to your chosen destination.

I can't choose your destination or your guiding principles for you. I wish I could, but they must be your own. But, when they are your own—when they are principles that you have established—they will be anchors that are strong and immovable.

I pray, Emily, that you will reach your hopes and dreams. I pray that you will have a happy and fulfilled life. Remember that I love you.

Love,
Grandpa Harry

He'd read it before but he still found it amazing. As he finished reading, he sat motionless staring at the screen.

Laura hated to interrupt his thoughts, and besides, the school was just around the corner. When she pulled against the curb and shut off the car, Bob turned, giving her a puzzled look.

"Sorry, I forgot to tell you. I promised Emily I'd pick her up today. She'll be out in about ten minutes. Now, you were saying?"

He paused for a moment. "It's just so strange. He was a crazy old man with Alzheimer's. How could he have done this?"

Laura was hesitant to say anything, to tell him what she'd discovered. After a moment, she decided now was as good a time as any.

"I need to tell you what I found."

"What?"

"I tracked down the pills—the ones I told you about. I talked to two doctors, Bob. The doctor who prescribed them was a friend of Harry's. Apparently Harry would stop by and visit on occasion. He was the one giving the pills to Harry."

"So, what did he tell you?"

"I never talked to him, he passed away over a year ago."

"What?"

"I spoke with his son, though. He's also a doctor. He looked up his dad's records and even remembered his dad speaking of Harry. The prescription was refilled by mail. It ran out a few months ago, about the time Harry started to get bad." Bob was interested. She continued. "Harry probably suffered from the early stages of Alzheimer's. But his prescription was to treat depression. The doctor's notes showed that Harry had suffered from it for a very long time—many years—perhaps his entire life."

"But the clinic, they said he had AD?"

"I've been to the clinic. You should see it. It makes the Department of Motor Vehicles look good. They run the elderly through and they make the easy diagnosis, the one that gives them the most Medicare money. They didn't run any tests for chemical imbalance, depression, or any kind of mental illness—not one. I had a doctor check. I'm not saying Harry was 'crazy,' just that he suffered from some sort of depression. Did you know it affects more than twenty million adults in the United States?"

She had expected him to argue or get angry. Instead he seemed reflective.

"So when did he write this stuff, Laura?"

"I'm guessing he wrote a little while each day. He could have been working on it for years. Who knows? Your dad was a hard person to figure out. In many ways he didn't share a lot of himself. Perhaps he couldn't. I honestly don't know. I think his poems are his best effort to let us know he was trying—that he cared."

The car's rear door swung open. "Daddy?"

"Hey, Emily."

"What are you doin' here?"

"Were you expecting Leonardo DiCaprio?"

"Who?"

"Never mind. How's my girl doing?"

"Good, but why are you here?"

"I came for a few days to take care of some stuff—Harry's things."

"You're not staying?"

"For a little bit, honey. What do you say we go to a movie and dinner?"

"Right now?"

"Sure, if it's okay with your mother. My treat."

Laura rolled her eyes. "What? Like I have a choice now?"

Emily noticed that Bob carried Harry's book. While they drove toward the mall, she asked him to read her some of the poems. Bob read aloud for everyone to hear. One in particular caught Emily's attention.

"I know that one."

"What do you mean you know it?" Bob inquired.

"I know the answer. It's the same as the horse joke."

"What are you talking about, child?" Laura added.

"Read it again and I'll show you." Emily was suddenly the center of attention and Laura could tell that she liked it. She would drag this out as long as she could. Bob read the poem again.

My name is so boring, said old farmer Fred.
"I'll liven the barnyard," that odd farmer said. "I'll name all my animals, oh, what a fun game. I'll think up unusual, odd sort of names."

The dog he named "Mohama," I think it's from Tonga, the pig's name was "Squarky," the duck, "Cuckamonga." The cow, "Woble-Mable," the goat he called "Jama," even the frog by the pond, "Lillyrama."

The cat he called "Pawzer," the sheep, "Woolsy-Woo," the horse in the stable was now "Mala-paloo." And not just the animals, I know it seems funny, but even his wife he called "Sweetie-pie-honey."

There's just one I've not mentioned, he's old and he's lame. It's the old tired mule, Fred's hidden his name. This game may seem silly, some even say cruel. Now guess if you can what is the name of the mule.

"Did Harry read a lot of Dr. Seuss?" Bob questioned.

"I was wondering the same thing," Laura admitted.

"He is clever though. I tried each animal name back-wards. I put them all together. Nothing has worked."

Emily giggled. "Yep, it's just the same as the horsy joke."

"Do you care to share it with us, or do you not want a movie after all?" Laura teased.

"Okay, it's a riddle that Grandpa used to tell me. It goes . . .

I once owned a horse
He won great fame
What-do-you-guess
Was the horse's name?

"Don't you get it? The horse was named 'What-do-you-guess.' "

Laura and Bob both looked at each other in amazement. It was so silly, yet right there in front of their faces. Bob clicked on the file and typed in the name of the mule— "Nowguessifyoucanwhat." To his surprise, the file opened. "Okay, here it goes."

Dearest Emily,

I will never forget a story my father once told. I suppose it was a fable told to him by his father. Teach it to your children as well.

Once upon a time there was a farmer who owned a mule. The mule was old and was losing his sight. One day the mule stumbled into an abandoned well that lay on the farm. He was shaken by the fall but not hurt, and as he attempted to get out of the well he began to bray. The old mule made so much noise that the farmer rushed to the well to find out what the commotion was about. The well was deep and the mule was old. The farmer figured the mule was injured and decided that the most prudent action would be to bury the old mule right then and there. The farmer retrieved a shovel from the barn and began shoveling the old well full of dirt. The mule was confused and concerned about what was happening as dirt began to land on his head and back. It appeared, Emily, that it was the end of him, until an amazing thing happened. Each time a shovel full of dirt fell onto his back, he shook it off and stomped it into the ground beneath him. The more dirt that fell, the more he shook and stomped. By the end of the day, he'd shaken and stomped long enough that even though the well did fill up, he stayed on top. With the well sufficiently full, he stepped out and walked, exhausted, to his stall in the barn.

I don't mean to compare you to an old mule, Emily, but, in life, there will be people who will throw dirt on you. If you shake it off and don't let it build up, like that old mule, you'll be able to rise above those dark situations that will occur in your life.

Life is often difficult. But know also you will never be alone. When you feel a warm breeze on a cool summer evening and you suddenly remember me, I'll be there. When you've climbed as high as you possibly can climb and your body will go no farther, I'll be behind you to push you up one more step. When you fall, I'll be beneath you to soften the pain. You will not see me, but I will always be there.

I love you. Be good and always do the right thing.

Love,

Grandpa Harry

CHAPTER Sixteen

*G*REG AND MICHELLE ARRIVED ON THE MORNING FLIGHT. They rented a car and drove to the Denny's just off the freeway in Midvalley to meet Bob and Laura. It was a quick breakfast. Greg seemed anxious to get going.

Both cars pulled up in front of Harry's old brick house at the same time. Bob eyed Greg as he removed a long cardboard box from the trunk of his car. As he neared the steps, Bob could see it was a brand new metal detector. "Look close and I'll bet you can see dollar signs in his eyes," he muttered to Laura. She nudged him to be quiet.

"I picked this up from a specialty electronics store near the office," Greg announced, as he pulled it out of the box. "It's supposed to be state-of-the-art."

"Well, it ought to be, with all those buttons. Did they teach you how to use it?" Bob asked.

"It's easy. Let's start in the basement and I'll show you how it works."

The thought of Greg teaching him anything grated on Bob's nerves, but at the same time he was glad Greg had brought it. It would be horrible to sell the house, only to find out later that the new owners had discovered a stash of gold coins hidden somewhere inside.

Bob and Greg headed to the basement to start the search while the women sat comfortably at the kitchen table. They were supposed to be searching as well, but decided it was a job best left to the men and their electronic toy. "We'll just do what we do best," Michelle whispered to Laura. "Chat!"

As they usually visited only at Christmas, in many ways the two women felt like strangers. But today, Laura found it easy to talk to Michelle. The conversation started with information swapping about the children—Emily was in the second grade and loved her teacher—Michelle's kids were in fourth and sixth; Preston in soccer, and Devin in piano. They discussed jobs, neighbors, and clothing before Michelle mentioned Bob.

"I was just sick, Laura, when Bob told me you two were splitting up." She reached out and touched Laura on the leg. Laura wasn't sure what to say. Michelle continued, "And, just because he's my brother doesn't mean I think he's right. If you ask me, he's a fool."

Laura was appreciative of the support. "Thanks. I'll tell you, it can be so confusing at times. He comes back home and things seem to go well for a while, but then a few days or weeks later it's as though he were a different person; it just never seems to work out. In the long run, perhaps it's best." Several minutes passed before the door opened, and Greg and Bob entered the kitchen.

"Did you find anything?" Greg asked Michelle.

She smiled. "Not yet, dear, but as soon as we do, you'll be the first to know—and besides, you guys have the high-tech equipment. Does it work? Are we all rich yet?"

"Well, nothing yet," Greg replied briskly.

"Not exactly nothing," Bob interjected with a grin. "We did cut two holes in the wall before we figured out the metal detector's signals for copper plumbing pipe." He gave Laura a quick roll of the eyes.

"It's working great now," Greg continued. "Besides, the holes are behind the door. We can plug them easily."

"Well, don't let us stop you," Laura said. "We'll check again under the kitchen table in a minute." She gave Michelle a wink.

"On this floor," Bob began, "I think we should start in Harry's bedroom and work our way toward the front. What do you think?" He was trying to be civil. The truth was he couldn't have cared less what Greg thought. Both marched to the bedroom.

The room was still full of Harry's things. It made Bob feel like he was snooping where he didn't belong. Greg didn't seem to notice.

"Should we start in the closet?" Greg asked. He opened the arched door to the small closet and searched for a light inside. There was none. He guessed the closet was perhaps three feet wide and four feet deep. The floor was covered with a layer of crumpled socks and old shoes that looked so worn even Goodwill wouldn't want them.

After glancing at the pile on the floor, Greg chose to start with the ceiling. Bob watched as he moved the wand back and forth over the surface. The needles on the machine would occasionally bounce slightly, indicating that a nail or some other small piece of metal lay hidden beneath the surface. As Greg finished scanning the ceiling and walls, Bob wondered if they should move the old shoes so they could finish examining the floor. Greg simply ignored the mess, as he swept the disk over the top. Other than the plumbing pipes they'd discovered in the basement walls, the search had been fruitless. Now, we're scanning Harry's old shoes, Bob mused silently. At that moment, a screech blared from the machine that startled Bob. The alarm continued as he stepped forward to gaze at the machine that Greg held in his hand. The needles had moved all the way off the scales.

At the sound of the commotion, Laura and Michelle rushed into the room. The look in Greg's eyes was nothing short of triumphant. "I knew this detector would do the trick," he gloated. Bob could only nod. He hated to admit it, but Greg was right.

The closet was only big enough for one person at a time, so Laura and Michelle leaned on the bed, letting Bob and Greg maneuver for best position inside. Bob won. "Let's get these out of here," he suggested, eyeing the shoes and socks. Like a fire brigade passing buckets, Bob handed the shoes to Greg, who would in turn pass them off to Michelle and Laura, who would place them in a pile in the middle of the bed. Eight pairs of shoes, two strays that didn't seem to have matches, and seven assorted socks later, Bob emerged from the closet. He stood broadly in the doorway, letting Greg know he was not through inside. In his hand he held a wooden floor vent. "I think we've found something. There's an intake vent in the closet on the floor. It can't be a real vent."

"How would you know that?" Michelle wondered.

"First of all, you would never put an intake vent in a

closet. Vents need to be in a hall or big room for the air to circulate." Bob paused, trying to suppress a smile. "And secondly, when I reached in, I could feel the dial of a floor safe." Greg's smile broadened. Bob continued, "Laura, can you grab a flashlight from the basement for me?" He wasn't about to go himself and let Greg into the coveted spot.

"Sure, give me just a second."

A floor safe? The whole notion seemed bizarre, but at this point Bob would believe anything. "Do you remember this safe when we were kids, Michelle?" he questioned.

"I don't. Do you think it's been there that long?"

"Well, look at the vent cover. It looks pretty old. It's just surprising we didn't know about it. Then again, Harry was good at keeping things to himself," he added sarcastically.

Laura popped into the door with a flashlight in each hand. "Which one do you want?" She guessed he didn't care and handed him the biggest one. Bob snatched the light and then turned back into the closet. Greg squeezed in, attempting to hold the other light over Bob's head. The beams of light indeed revealed a large steel floor safe that had been hidden under the cover of the vent. It was about a foot and a half wide and almost as long. It was difficult to tell the age of the safe. It looked to Bob to be as old as the house, but then most safes look old, he reasoned. Either way, they had found it. Bob held the light in one hand and pulled on the handle with the other. The safe didn't budge. "The combination?" he muttered, as if someone outside the closet should know.

"Is there anything written on the door?" Greg asked.

"Nothing. There's nothing in here at all."

"How about the closet walls?"

Bob scanned the light slowly around the closet in all

directions while Greg tried to do the same. Again nothing. So close, yet without a combination they could not get inside. After several more seconds of searching, Bob decided it was time to retreat and let Greg have the closet to himself. The closeness was killing him, and he knew Greg wouldn't be happy until he checked every inch for himself. After a few minutes, Greg emerged. "Nothing."

"Like we didn't know that," Bob mumbled.

"There are usually three or four numbers. Let's check his desk, downstairs, anywhere he might have written it down. It must be here somewhere."

Forty minutes later, they had scoured the place and come up empty-handed. Greg was getting frustrated. He even checked every shoe from the closet.

"How about birthdays, social security numbers, anything?" Michelle and Laura began writing down all the important days, brainstorming any possibilities. Another half-hour later, they had dialed in every birthday, every anniversary, and even every death date. They tried them backwards and forwards. Greg would try them and then Bob would take a turn. Both were becoming short on patience. Michelle and Laura sat against the bed, while Bob and Greg sat on the floor near the closet.

"We could blast it open," Greg suggested.

"Oh, now there's a good idea," Bob replied.

"Okay then, I took welding in high school. How about we torch it open?" Bob could see this time Greg was serious.

"You can't torch open a safe. The walls are probably two inches thick. And besides, what if there's money inside? You want to burn it up? Not to mention the house."

"Can we get the whole thing out somehow? Get it out and then have it cut open?"

"Sure," Bob responded, tiring of Greg's stupid ideas, "We'll just cut a hole in the roof so the crane can lift it out. It must only weigh a thousand pounds."

Laura spoke next. "It seems to me that Harry wanted it hidden, at least for now. I'm guessing, but I'll bet the combination is hidden in one of his poems." Greg looked at Bob. They were thinking the same thing. "You get the books, I'll get paper. Everyone to the kitchen table."

Of the poems still not solved, it was easy to guess which one held the coveted combination. "It has to be the gold poem," Greg muttered. "And it's just not that complicated. If we all put our heads together, it shouldn't take long."

Sitting together as a group, Greg read it slowly aloud.

The Hidden Gold

Listen, a story I overheard told,
Of lost hidden treasure, tall mountains of gold.

Oh could it be true? Such a sight to behold,
Kings we would be with such piles of gold.

Assembled possessions were auctioned and sold,
To have enough money to search for the gold.

Health gone, their lives wasted, left tired and old,
Oh, life would've been grand, had we just found that gold.

Mirage? No it's there, just reach out and lay hold,
Each too blind to grasp the true nature of gold.

"If we all concentrate on this one poem," Michelle said, "it shouldn't take long to find the clue."

They had two books between them. Greg was the first to

notice it. "I think I have it. Yes, I do—it's similar to that other one, what was it, the floss one. Take the first letter of each line—it spells, 'Look at home.' I knew it!"

"Knew what?" Michelle wondered.

"That there's gold here. It tells us to look at home."

"Honey, I don't think it means that at all," Michelle replied.

Laura agreed. "Don't you see, Greg? It's a metaphor. Read the poem. He's saying one shouldn't waste a lifetime chasing after real gold because the true riches in life are, you know, happiness at home, that sort of thing."

"I guess I see your point, but it seems to me that it could read either way. Let's read the letter, see if we can find the combination, and then we'll know for sure."

Bob ran to the car to retrieve his laptop. When he returned, everyone gathered around the computer and watched the small screen.

Dearest Emily,

In life, remember the things that matter the most. It sounds so easy but is often difficult. Many of the problems we get worked up about don't matter. The sooner we come to that realization, the happier lives we'll live.

When we were to be married, Kathryn designed a beautiful wedding gown. She purchased some silk satin in San Francisco. It was ivory with a gold floral design woven through it. She spent hours working on the dress. It was almost complete when her mother came to town. Her mother was—well, let's just say a bit domineering. She insisted that her daughter wear a pure white gown and nothing else. I told Kathryn to stand up for herself, that it was her wedding, and that she should wear the dress she wanted. She was never one to back down from what she thought was right, so when she didn't seem concerned, I was puzzled. When I pressed her about it, she replied that certain things in life don't matter—it was just a dress, that she could wear a flour sack to her wedding and as long as we were still husband and wife afterwards, she'd be happy.

The wedding day arrived and she did wear a plain white dress. She taught me a great lesson that day. Unfortunately, it took me many years to understand that lesson fully. You see, Emily, I was hoping that when Michelle married, she'd wear that gold dress as a tribute to Kathryn. Instead, Michelle ran off and got married without even telling me. I was furious. I couldn't even speak to her for months. It took me that long to realize that I was being just as bullheaded as Kathryn's mother—it was, after all, just a dress.

I'd always wanted to apologize to Michelle, tell her that I was wrong. I didn't get around to it. The more time that passed, the harder it became. Learn from my mistake, Emily. If you hurt someone, tell them right away that you're sorry and move on with your life. It gets harder as time passes.

Oddly, Kathryn never kept the dress, the white one she actually wore on her wedding day. When a friend needed a dress for her wedding, Kathryn gave her the dress and told her she didn't need it back. The gold dress, however, she cherished. I think, to her, the gold dress was her wedding gown. She tried it on occasionally, but most of the time it sat, boxed carefully, in the top of the closet.

I gave a piece of the dress to you, by the way. Look at the cover of your book and you will find it. Now I know that the thought of your old grandpa cutting up Kathryn's beloved dress will make Bob and Michelle cringe. When they do, put your little arms around their necks, squeeze them tight, and tell them that your grandpa learned the hard way that it's only a dress; it doesn't really matter.

You had a wonderful grandmother. I can't wait for the day when you get to meet her.

Love,

Grandpa Harry

"I never knew he wanted me to wear it. I'd have loved to. I'm sorry," Michelle whispered.

"Don't apologize," Laura replied. "You didn't know."

"Why did you two just run off anyway?" Bob questioned.

"Bob?" Laura winced at his words, hoping Greg and Michelle wouldn't be offended.

"No, it's okay," Michelle continued. "I thought Dad hated Greg."

"He did hate me," Greg added.

"Well, that's true," she continued with a smile. "I was young and scared. I figured if I told Dad, he wouldn't let me go through with it. We'd only known each other for a few weeks. So we just ran off."

"I don't blame you," Bob added. "Except I didn't have anyone to talk to after that."

"Hey, I don't mean to interrupt this fun little jaunt down memory lane here, but let me remind everyone, we still don't have a combination to the safe." Michelle rolled her eyes at Greg's cold comment. Bob knew he was right.

As she contemplated the problem, Laura was struck with an idea. "What about the one you read to me coming home from the airport, Bob? The password was all numbers and the title was something about safety in numbers. Could he be saying 'Safe Numbers'?"

Bob's eyes widened. "That's a good idea, Laura." He marveled at her astuteness. The poem was quickly located. The numbers were two, ten, and eighty-two.

"It won't work," Bob realized, sitting back down at the table.

"And why not, little brother?" Michelle questioned.

"Eighty-two is too large. There's no eighty-two on the dial. It was a good idea though."

Just to be sure Greg ran to the safe and dialed in two, ten, eight, and then two. The handle didn't budge.

"Sorry," Laura apologized as he walked back to the table. "It was just a thought."

"At least she's thinking," Michelle added. "I guess then it must still be hidden in another poem."

Tired, they continued to scour the remaining poems for clues. After another thirty minutes, Laura glanced at her watch. She had just two more hours before she'd need to leave to get Emily. Michelle interrupted the silence, "I think I have it."

"You do?" Greg's eyes were wide with excitement.

"I don't know if it will tell us what we need, but check out the grammar poem—you know, the one on page twenty-two. Look at how clever." She read the poem to the group.

The Writer's Dilemma

Proper English is important, my dear parents taught to me;
It will help you get through college, get a job, trust us, you'll see.

It's not that I don't believe them, I don't mean to stew and fret;
It's just English is perplexing, there are things that I don't get.

In choosing words to share ideas, I try to be selective;
I'm just confused, that noun I used, is it abstract or collective?

And words combined to make just one, I think they're called
conjunctions;
And expletives used properly, just what the hell's their function?

And words have gender, yes, it's true, like sister, aunt or gent;
If they're used wrong, can I be sued, for sexual harassment?

My ad-verbs never seem to add, and adjectives I mangle;
Do I need to call the doctor, when my participles dangle?

I hope you understand my plight. Don't think my view absurd;
It seems my best solution is, shut up, don't say a word!

Yet grammar, like most everything, the more you try, you grow;
Now simply solve the riddle, just think and read it slow.

Tomorrow soon will be today, today soon gone forever;
What's done is done, so don't be tense, these words are not that clever.

"So what's the password?" Greg asked.

Michelle was thrilled to have been the one to find it. "Well, the poem is about grammar and he comes right out and tells us that the solution to the riddle is in the last stanza. He's very quick-witted."

"Get to the point, Michelle." Greg's patience was gone.

"I am. You see, he tells us not to be tense about the verbiage. You get it? He's asking us for the three verb tenses— the ones you learn in grammar school. 'Tomorrow soon will be today' is the future, 'today is gone forever' is the present, and 'what's done is done' certainly describes the past.

Bob typed in the words. She was right. It opened instantly. He turned the screen toward Michelle to let her read.

Dearest Emily,

I want to talk to you now about hopes, dreams, reality, and choice. As you grow and mature, you will start to create a vision of your life. Dreams will blossom and grow. This is good. Without dreams, we would lose hope. Just remember to keep them in perspective.

What I am saying is that some of your dreams will come true, others will fade or change, and others will be dashed to pieces before your eyes. You will probably need to let go of a dream or two in your life, but as you do, other opportunities will blossom before you.

As a young man, I loved to write poems. I don't remember when I started. They always seemed to be a part of me. I would use them to express the deepest feelings of my heart, something I find difficult to do face-to-face.

After my graduation from college, I took a job at a newspaper in El Paso, Texas. We packed up everything we owned, climbed into our old car, and drove to Texas to begin our life. The job lasted just two months before the paper folded, laying off all of its employees. I started my search for another position—there weren't many. Before I began, however, Kathryn convinced me that I should compile some of my poems into a book and send them off for publication.

I will admit to you now that since childhood I'd dreamed of becoming a famous writer. I was enthralled by her confidence in me. I was excited and yet nervous, all at the same time. Kathryn worked as a secretary during the day, and as a seamstress at night to support us, while I spent my days and nights writing my first book of poems.

I poured my heart and soul into the book and was so proud when it was finished. The first rejection letter was devastating. I was expressing my innermost dreams, hopes, and desires to the world and found the world had trampled on them. By the time the rejections numbered a dozen, I was completely numb. After two dozen rejections I sat down on the back porch and reevaluated my priorities. It was a diffi-cult thing to do. How long does the actress wait tables before giving up hope of getting her first part? How many times does the violin player audition before realizing he may never be a part of the symphony? When does the dancer hang up her shoes, realizing her moves are not as graceful as those of younger girls on the stage?

I began to think of Kathryn and her dream of living in a redbrick house, with arched doorways—a tree swing in the side yard and a front porch where she could sit in the evening and wave to the neighbors as they'd pass.

On my current path, I could see it was likely that we'd never reach that dream. Ultimately, I accepted a position with an advertising company in Lake Park. We saved every penny, and soon had enough to begin our home in Midvalley. My brother, Arty, helped me build the house. We swung our hammers side by side as the house took shape. I promised him I'd return the favor and help him build a house as soon as he married, but I never got the chance. He died in a smelter accident just three years later.

In many ways, Emily, I felt I gave up a chance at my dream of being a poet for that of a lesser dream. And yet, there would be days when I'd watch Kathryn sitting on the front porch, sewing and waving to all the neighbors, and I'd wonder if it wasn't the greater dream after all.

Follow your dreams, make your best choices, and peace will come as you realize that you are on the best path for yourself. Your journey is unique. What is nourishment to others, may in fact be poison to you. Have dreams, but be content with your journey.

Before I end for today, I need to tell you that I was finally published, in a manner of speaking. In my employment at Allsop & Martin Advertising, I handled the outdoor advertising accounts of several national customers. I'll bet you had no idea that your Grandpa Harry coined the slogan, "No Awful Waffles at Willy's." It was the longest-running billboard campaign for any restaurant in the company's history.

Live your potential, Emily. Reach for your dreams and then celebrate your joy when you achieve success. I'll be watching you.

Love,

Grandpa Harry

Greg spoke first. "I'm curious. Why'd he write these to Emily?"

Laura tried to apologize. "They were best friends. I brought her to visit Harry every Friday. I'm sure if you had lived nearby he would have written letters to all the grandchildren."

"Don't misunderstand. I'm not complaining, just curious."

"It's beautiful advice for anyone. I just wonder, why now?" Michelle added.

Laura answered. "I'm guessing, Michelle, it was Harry. For some reason he couldn't tell you and Bob how he felt. I think this is his one last chance to let everyone know—that he did care."

"Still no combination. Any ideas now?"

"Greg!" Michelle chided.

"Just trying to get the job done that we came to do."

Laura checked her watch again. "You all keep working on

it. I'll go over to Subway and grab some sandwiches." Bob agreed that was a great idea. He hadn't had much for breakfast and he was starving.

The Subway shop was just a few blocks away. She'd often dropped by with Emily on Fridays after visiting Harry. She didn't know the help by name, but the two girls working today looked familiar. She placed her order with one and then watched as the other began to prepare the sandwiches. While Laura waited, her mind pondered the poems. There was one other poem that mentioned gold. Could that be the one? If Harry had wanted them to find the safe, wouldn't he have told them where to find it?

"That will be eighteen dollars and ninety cents." Laura snapped out of her daydream and rummaged for a twenty-dollar bill from her purse. "Here you go," she declared, handing the money to the young girl.

"Thank you, ma'am." The girl punched the cash register and retrieved the change. Like most cashiers, she stated the total and then counted the change backwards as she dropped it into Laura's hand. "Eighteen ninety, nineteen, and a dollar makes twenty."

The words sounded familiar. "What did you say?"

"I'm sorry, did I count that wrong?" She picked up the change from Laura's hand and began to count again. Laura wasn't watching. She was in another world. The girl recounted. "Your total was eighteen ninety. Your change is a dime, which makes nineteen, and then a dollar makes twenty. It's correct." Laura grinned. "You are a clever one, Harry," she pronounced aloud as she handed the change back to the girl. "Here, thanks so much."

When she entered the house, Bob and Greg sat dejected, elbows on the table, staring blankly at the pages before them. Michelle was casually flipping through the poems, her attention and patience long gone.

"I know something you don't know," Laura teased as she entered the room with the sandwiches.

"What would that be?" Bob wondered, glancing up only briefly from the book.

"I know the solution. The girl at the Sub shop helped me out."

Both Bob and Greg perked up, though Bob seemed confused. "The girl at the Sub shop knew Harry?"

"I have no idea if she knew Harry, but she helped me figure it out." They stared motionless as she continued, "There's one other poem that mentions gold." She picked up the book and began to search for a particular page. "Let's see—yes, it's poem eighteen. Anyone want to read it first?" she questioned. Greg was there and started immediately.

We Must Change

I watched with shock as Evening News
*   showed ravages of war;*
Of orphan child in distant lands,
*   the plight of working poor.*
He told of crime increasing,
*   of violent acts untold;*
Does no one care 'bout fellow men?
Are all just seeking gold?

Sickened at the baneful world,
*   I walked the street alone;*
Is all faith lost, is hope now gone?

Have men's hearts turned to stone?
The world must change for any hope
of better life someday;
But millions here are hard and cold,
pain seems our destined way.

With heavy heart and downcast soul,
I glanced across the road;
A homeless man sat begging,
lonely, weak, and cold.
I usually cross to the other side,
ignoring beggar's plight;
I know not why, I walked to him,
"Please, may I help tonight?"

With voice soft spoke, his eyes cast down,
"Sir, can you spare some change?"
His words they echoed deep within,
I felt my heart beat strange.
He asked for "change," the simple word,
struck deep with power and might;
"Come walk with me, let's get you fed,
we'll both get change tonight."

I walked with him to buy a meal,
we sat and talked, two brothers;
"I thank you sir, your act was kind,
I will repay another."
Five twenty-five is all it cost,
to feed that friend in need;
I left a ten, said "Keep the change,"
my answer strong indeed.

That simple word, it starts inside,
  it echoes strong and clear;
The world can change, it starts with us,
  those eyes there in the mirror.
We change ourselves, then others see
  the light within our soul;
We set the first example;
  they will see the higher goal.

The key then sounds so simple,
  it resonates so strange;
It starts with us, then moves the world,
  the simple act of change.

"Okay," Bob chimed in, "the anticipation is killing me. How'd the girl at the Sub shop help you?"

"I'd been reading the poem earlier. It was the way she counted the change. It just clicked."

Bob looked puzzled. Laura continued, "The poem is about change, right? Changing ourselves to make a better world. But in the poem he buys the man food for five twenty-five—he gives him a ten and tells him to keep the change. The whole poem is about change. I'll bet if you take the change from the poem—four seventy-five, you'll find your answer."

Greg's jaw dropped open. Laura continued. "And the password is a number. Try four, seven, and then five."

Bob turned to Greg. "I'll race you to the closet."

"I'm right behind you."

Bob dialed in the numbers and grasped the handle firmly. Greg held the light. Bob paused, anticipating the moment, before giving the handle a jerk. It didn't move.

"Try it again." Still nothing. They walked out and glared at Laura as if it were her fault. She simply shrugged.

"Wait!" Bob shouted, tossing his hands into the air. "'Four-seventy-five' is the password to the letter. Why are we trying it on the safe?" He raced to the computer and opened the file.

> Dearest Emily,
> I want to talk to you about money.

"I knew it," Greg interjected. Bob continued.

> As I'm prone to do, let me start with a story. When I was a boy of about seven or eight, I found a stray dog one day on my way home from school. He was an abandoned mutt, but to a young boy, what a terrific mutt he was. I named him Chester and we became inseparable. I left him only to go to school. (I even tried to sneak him into class once, but the teacher called my parents. I received a good whipping when I got home and had to promise never to take him to school again.)
>
> One day I discovered a small sore under Chester's right eye. As days passed, other sores started to appear under his hair and around his ears. I knew my dad would never spend money on a stray, so on my own I tried washing the sores every day with soap. The condition became worse. When I finally approached my father, I guess my desperation was evident; he never argued. He looked at me and then at the dog, and without even asking a question, he instructed me to get the dog and meet him in the car.
>
> We drove to town where the veterinarian lived. The doctor took one look at the sores and knew immediately what

was wrong. He went to his cabinet and took out a box of pills—medicine that would cure my dog's condition. He didn't seem extremely concerned, but instructed me to give him one pill each morning and one each evening for the first three weeks and then one pill each morning for the following three weeks. He told me to bring the dog back in six weeks, if the condition didn't clear up.

I was thrilled. My dog was going to be okay. I gave him the first pill that very night, and then the second the next morning before school. In my haste to leave that morning, I left the box containing the pills on my desk, rather than putting it away inside the drawer. They must have been made to taste good, at least to dogs, because sometime during the day, Chester jumped up onto the desk, chewed open the package, and ate every one of the pills.

I came home from school to find him asleep on the floor of my bedroom. He never woke up. The medicine that would have slowly made him better, taken all at once, took his life instead.

I apologize for telling such a sad story, but the moral fits so many aspects of our lives, including money. Riches can be used to enrich and bless our lives just like the medicine, but if taken or used foolishly, the effects can be disastrous.

Many people think that money is bad or evil. It isn't. Others think that if they have a lot of it, they will be happy. They won't. Still others believe that if they have more of it than people around them, they will be better. They aren't. And yet, it's a paradox, because we must eat. Money, used as a means of barter, helps us in that goal. It isn't inherently good or bad, just part of the whole process of working for our sustenance.

The difficult question then, Emily, is knowing how much is enough. If a man does nothing but stay home and play with his children, soon those children will be hungry, because there will be no money to purchase food. If the same man works all the time to earn money to provide food, the children will not want for food, but will instead develop a greater hunger, the need for a father. The balance must plainly lie somewhere in between. Where is the balance for you? It is a question I cannot answer—only you can. My hope is to bring the dilemma to your attention—help you find the answer for yourself.

I have two presents for you, Emily. Take the book of poems you are reading and untie the ribbon on the back inside cover. If you do, the cover will slide open and you will find a gold coin. This coin is for you. It represents the money and gold you will seek during your life. It is new, it is bright, and it is valuable. You may do with it what you choose.

Your choices are many. You could keep it; if you do it may tarnish and fade, or it may become even more valuable. You could spend it, buying something to make your life easier or enjoyable. You could invest it wisely, perhaps increasing it a hundredfold. You could lose it and end up with nothing. You could give it to another in need to lighten his burden.

As with the coin, your choices in life will be many— weigh them carefully; consider their consequences. Over the years, the thousands of choices you make, bundled together, will show what you value.

Now, here is the most important part to remember— choice in life is not between wealth and poverty, nor is it between fame and obscurity. Choice in life is between good and evil. When you understand this lesson, material things will not determine your happiness. The great irony in life is that the world's richest man and the world's poorest man *will stand side by side in front of God with exactly the same amount.*

That said, I have much more for you than a single gold coin. My desire is to give you incredible riches. They are hidden in a safe in the floor of my closet. There you will find gold worth much more than just the coin hidden in the book. Consider what I have said and make your choices wisely.

Love,

Grandpa Harry

I almost forgot to tell you the combination. Wouldn't that have been funny? The combination is 1, 2, 3. Ridiculous I know, but it was the only way I could remember.

"One, two, three?" Greg repeated in disbelief. They headed for the closet.

This time as Bob dialed in the combination and jerked the handle, it turned with a clank. Greg wanted to high-five everyone but instead kept his composure. The lid was heavy but lifted back to stay open. Shining the light over Bob's head, Greg could see three boxes inside wrapped in brown paper. Bob reached in and lifted them out with ease. A quick glance inside revealed that to be everything in the safe.

"I hope it's money, 'cause it isn't heavy enough to be gold," Bob announced. Greg tried not to look disappointed. Bob pushed the pile of shoes to the foot of the bed and placed the boxes in the center. They were wrapped like Christmas gifts but in plain brown paper. Bob stepped back to stare.

"What are we waiting for?" Michelle questioned. She picked up one of the boxes and handed it to Laura. "We'll do it together." Laura smiled as they both began to unwrap the gifts. Under the paper was a cardboard box with the lid taped closed. Laura ran her nail over the tape to pop open the lid. Inside was gold indeed—an intricately carved gold picture frame held a photograph of a young couple. It took Laura a moment to recognize it as Harry and Kathryn. She had never seen the picture and it was mesmerizing. They both looked so young, and Harry so different from the man she had known. They were holding hands. She studied it closely. Kathryn beamed and indeed she was beautiful.

"This is fantastic," Laura announced. "Have you ever seen this picture?" Bob and Michelle both shook their heads. Michelle had opened her box and it held an identical frame and picture. She whispered, "Dad had very few pictures of Mom. I've never seen this one. It is incredible."

"Do you think Harry made the frames?" Laura wondered.

"I doubt it," Bob replied.

But as Laura turned the picture over, the initials H. W. were carved into one corner. "Yes, look, his initials are on the back."

"But, there's no gold?" Greg asked, unable to hide his dejection.

"Don't you see, Greg?" Laura responded. "There is gold—just like in the poem—it's a different kind. Harry is trying to tell us that family and love are worth infinitely more than any gold coin."

Greg nodded, pretending to appreciate the analogy. "Wait!" he declared as his eyes brightened at a sudden thought. "Most safes have a false back or hidden drawer." He grabbed a flashlight and headed to the closet to check.

"Give it up, Greg. There isn't any more gold," Michelle responded.

"Just give me a second," he called from the closet. "Yes, there is a hidden back!" Pulling on a small fabric tab, the felt-covered back panel of the safe pulled out. Greg swung around, handed it to Bob and then headed again to the back of the closet. Reaching inside the small compartment, he removed two letters. He kept fishing, but that was everything the safe contained.

He crawled from the closet looking dejected. "Two letters. That's it." He handed them to Bob, and turned back into the closet for one last look, just to be sure.

"Can I see them, Bob?" Laura questioned, taking the first letter from him to examine it more closely. The envelope had yellowed and the paper was crisp; otherwise it was in perfect condition. It was addressed to Kathryn at an address in Denver. Sliding the letter from its envelope, she began to read it aloud.

My Dearest Kathryn,

I pray this letter finds you in good spirits. I hope you arrived without incident. I also hope that my inability to write what I feel will not hinder you from seeing into my heart. I wish that I were skilled in writing, that with a few strokes of a pen I could portray the feelings that burn in my heart.

My heart is about to break as I fear that I may have driven you away forever. I have been racked with such terrible torment since you left. I was so foolish in the things that I said. Sometimes I act so stupidly.

I stared into the hallway mirror on the night that you left, but I did not recognize the pathetic man staring back. I cannot explain the things that I said, because there is no reasonable explanation. Instead, I hope you will realize they were not my words but rather those of a stranger.

If you choose not to return, I will understand. Your

absence will be of my own doing. But at the same time my existence will be utterly miserable without you by my side. I will shiver, for you are my warmth—I will be lonely, for you are my friend—I will be lost, for you are my guide. Everything good in me, no matter how small, you discover. I long to see your smile in the morning, to feel your touch in the evening.

Please, Kathryn, return and grant me your forgiveness. I will be anxiously awaiting your reply.

With all my love,

Harry

No one spoke as Laura finished. Even Greg sat quietly. Laura's voice broke the silence. "This is the most beautiful letter I've ever read."

"I wonder what he did to make her leave?" Bob asked. "From the way Harry always described it, they were Romeo and Juliet." Bob had no memory of his mother. As a child he'd often longed for a whisper of her image, the shimmer of her hair, the glance of her smile.

"I'm guessing there was quite a bit that we didn't know," Michelle replied.

Laura turned the envelope over and read the postmark: May 9, 1965.

Michelle spoke softly, "That was just a few days before her death."

"She was killed in a car accident, wasn't she?" Greg questioned.

"Yes, honey, near the park, not far from here. I've told you that."

Bob stared at the postmark. "Were you and I with her in Denver, Michelle?"

"I don't remember being in Denver," she replied.

"Wait, tell me again what you do remember about the accident."

Michelle closed her eyes. "You were just a baby. You were in the back. I had to be three or four. I don't remember many details. It was dusk. I remember laughing about something and then the car was rolling over. That's it. The next thing that I recall, I was playing at home."

"Do you remember playing in the park before the ride home?" Bob wondered. Michelle looked pensive.

"I can't say. I thought that I did, since that's what Dad had always told us, but honestly, I just can't remember."

When he or Michelle had asked Harry about the accident, they were always told the same story; the accident occurred on the way home from the park. As children, they'd had no reason to question what their father told them.

"What are you saying Bob?" Laura asked, "Do you think she was coming home from Denver and not from the park?"

Bob shrugged. "I'm not sure what to think."

"I hope not." Laura voiced with concern. "I hope that she made it back home before the accident. Harry deserved a second chance."

"What does the other letter say?" Greg inquired.

Turning it over, Laura could see it had never been opened. "It's still sealed, and look at the address." It had been addressed to Kathryn Whitney. Underneath her name, in place of an address, was scribbled the word *Heaven*.

"Heaven?" questioned Bob. "That's crazy."

"No, it's touching," Laura replied. "Look, it was mailed two months after her death—and look at the postmark." With no proper address, the letter had been returned by the post office with large red letters stamped below the word, Heaven. They read, "Return to Sender—No such address."

"No such address?" Bob mused. "Like anyone at the post office would know."

"Should we open it?" Laura wondered.

"Well, I hardly think anybody is going to press charges if we do," Bob replied sarcastically.

Grabbing a letter opener from the desk, Laura cut open the top of the envelope and let the letter slide out. "I don't think I can read it after the last one. Michelle, it's your turn." Michelle passed the letter to Greg, knowing he'd get through it just fine. He shrugged and began to read.

My Dearest Kathryn,

I know you are in Heaven for there is no other place good enough. I know you must be there, but I don't know how to let you know that I am sorry. When you died, I died as well. I can't eat. I can't sleep. I can't continue without you.

How can I find you to tell you that I am . . .

"That's it—he never finished it. It isn't even signed."

"And it still doesn't say if she made it back," Laura continued. "And if she didn't—if she died on her way home—I hate to think what Harry went through."

Everyone considered the implications.

Greg and Bob searched the rest of the house, just to be sure. They found nothing else. Harry's shoes were stacked neatly back into the closet; it didn't feel right clearing them out today. Laura gave Michelle a quick hug and waited in the car; Bob found himself standing on the porch alone with his sister.

"It wasn't as bad as you remember, Bob," Michelle whispered. "I think perhaps we just missed having a mother."

"You could be right." He seemed reflective for only a moment, before he smiled to hide his emotions. "But, hey, it's over. Nothing we can do to change the past now."

She looked into his eyes; he turned away. "We can't change things, Bob, but are they really over?"

He stayed silent. She wouldn't push any further.

"We can stay another day to help clean out Dad's things."

"No reason to, Sis. I'm guessing Greg is anxious to get back. We'll get everything wrapped up. Just send me a list of the things you want from the house and I'll ship them out to you."

Bob knew he didn't need much—just a few things for Emily—to help her remember.

He hugged his sister good-bye and then waved at Greg, who waited in the car. Before locking the door to Harry's house, he stepped back inside, wrapped up his gold-framed picture, and carefully carried it out to the car.

CHAPTER *Seventeen*

℘MILY WAS THRILLED WITH THE FIND. SHE INSISTED BOB find a nail and hang her new picture on the wall above her desk. It matched the surroundings perfectly.

After Laura tucked Emily securely in bed with both blankets, she took the first turn to lie down with her. Bob was in the kitchen when the phone rang.

"Bob, is that you?"

"Michelle? Where are you?"

"We're on our way back home. They had seats on the evening flight. I'm on the air-phone. I've never used one of these before. Isn't technology great?"

"Is there a problem?"

"Not at all. Just found another password. Thought you'd like to know. When are you heading back?"

"In the morning."

"Are you sure, little brother, you can't work things out with Laura?"

"Michelle, everyone has their own set of circumstances—things they have to deal with—their own perspectives. It may not seem like it, but I know what I am doing."

She knew from experience that it was pointless to argue. Bob thanked her again and jotted down the password. After lying down with Emily, and kissing her goodnight, he grabbed Harry's book and called Laura to the kitchen.

"It's the parent poem, Laura. Here's the funny part. There's nothing hidden really. It's the phrase that's repeated at the end of each verse. I can't believe we didn't try it before now."

Laura opened the book and read the poem.

Parents

I love you, will you marry me?
It was "*I*," but now it's "*we*."
Romantic nights. Time for fun.
One in the oven, soon to be done.
Could you get me a pickle, sliced on a plate?
We should have stayed home from that very first date.
Hospital bills. New kid to be fed.
Money for fun, buying diapers instead.
                    And time goes by . . .

Mom-ma, Dad-da. First words spoken.
First steps taken. Dishes broken.
A spoonful for Daddy, open wide,
Climb on my back, it's a horsy ride.
More spilt milk. Try not to yell.
Please don't pull the doggie's tail.

Your turn for the diaper. Your turn to cook.
Did you see where I put the Dr. Spock book?
And time goes by . . .

Disneyland and Mickey Mouse.
Training pants. *Let's play house.*
Potty trained. *Oh, Happy Day!*
Guess what? Another one's on the way.
I wet the bed. My goldfish died.
You want to seek, if I go hide?
Kindergarten. Chicken pox.
Go outside, but don't throw rocks.
And time goes by . . .

Did you brush your teeth, and say your prayers?
Tell me the story of the three little bears.
Run and get dressed. *There's no underwear.*
I got Mommy's scissors and cut my own hair!
Wash your face. Now, no more tears.
But who's gonna check behind my ears?
Dressed as broccoli for the school play.
President of the PTA.
And time goes by . . .

I'll be at my friends. Did you make your bed?
I got my report card. Tonight, I'm dead.
Lots of laughter, add some tears.
How will they handle pressure from peers?
I have a question, where are babies from?
I'm busy now, go ask your mom.

The dog ate my homework, I still got an A.
Girl Scout leader. Nervous breakdown today.
                              And time goes by . . .

My first date! I've got nothing to wear.
Beauty cream. It's a bad day for hair.
This is Ashley. This is Brad.
Be home by twelve. *Don't listen to Dad.*
Paying the bills, don't ask me how.
Buying hairspray by the gallon now.
You're awesome Dad. You guys are so mean.
I was elected Homecoming Queen!
                              And time goes by . . .

After you pee, put down the lid!
I'm sorry Mom, I thought I did.
My nose is so big and my hips are too wide.
It's from Grandma Henry on your mother's side.
Midlife crisis. Pants getting too tight.
My head really hurts dear, so please not tonight.
Can I have the keys? Did you mow the lawn?
Who's your new friend? *Dad, come and meet Dawn.*
                              And time goes by . . .

Graduating from college, a wedding to plan.
Does your friend with spiked hair have to be the best man?
I call with great news, I'm expecting in June.
Isn't it great, you'll be grandparents soon!
I'm old, I forget, did we teach them to cook?
Mom, can I borrow that Dr. Spock book?

The house finally quiet, enough of this rhyme.
The kids are all gone. It's vacation time!

By the time Laura had finished, Bob already had the letter open and printed. He handed it to Laura. "Do you want to read it or do you want me to?"

"I don't mind." She started to read.

Dearest Emily,

Parents are strange and wonderful creatures. When you're small they seem bright, shiny, and invincible. As you grow, that image starts to fade. It's a sobering moment, but the time will come when you realize they are not the heroes you imagined. They are just people struggling to do the best they can, just the same as you are. You will feel let down, betrayed, even ashamed. This is the time, Emily, when you need to forgive your parents for being human. Let me tell you a story that will help you understand.

When your daddy was young, just four to be exact, he loved to climb the trees in the backyard. It was something to behold, watching his confidence grow as each day he would climb higher and higher into their branches. Soon, no tree seemed too high or too scary.

One Saturday I was in the house doing some writing. To my horror, I heard Bobby begin to scream like a maniac. I jumped to my feet, knocking over my chair, and bolted for the back door. I was sure he'd cut off a finger or broken an arm. As I burst through the door, I could see him hanging in the willow on the far corner of the lot. Though it was smaller then, it was still a good-sized tree. He had shimmied out onto a branch and then must have slipped, because he was holding on by his hands, his feet dangling. He was losing his grip and screaming like he was about to drop into a bed of hot lava. The funny part is that he wasn't very high off the ground, perhaps six feet or so.

I ran beneath him and reached up to grab his legs, letting him know I was there and it would be all right. The feel of my touch and the sound of my voice reassured him; he let go, sliding down into my grasp. He hugged me so tightly, I thought he would strangle me. At only four, he was still too young to worry about hiding emotions in front of his dad. As he sobbed and sighed with relief, he thanked me for saving him.

At that moment, he believed I could do anything. I was there when he needed me. It was such a simple moment, but one I'll cherish till the day I die. Nothing seemed impossible; I was a superhero; I had saved my son.

But children grow, Emily. The years pass; children become bigger and the trees seem smaller. Soon they are jumping down from the same branches with ease.

When your dad was twelve, he fell again from the very same tree. This time I wasn't there to catch him and he didn't land on his feet. As he hit the ground, his arm snapped in two places. I was out of town on business and when I arrived home the next day, he was sitting on the couch, his arm in a cast. Still in pain, he explained how he fell from the branch I'd saved him from as a child. He didn't say it, perhaps he didn't even think it, but he knew that I had failed him. I wasn't there. I think he felt I'd let him down. I think that day, my shining armor tarnished, even if unconsciously, in his eyes. It was not my fault; it was not his fault; it was just part of life.

There are times, however, when your parents should be standing under the tree to catch you, but they won't be. Parents make mistakes, sometimes big ones. I don't think this will make sense to you now, but Emily, there will come a time when

you will have to forgive your parents for not being there when
you fall out of the tree.

The day you do, you will begin to forget their mistakes and
their armor will once again shine a little brighter in your eyes.
I hope someday that you will understand.

   Love,
   Grandpa Harry

Laura stared at Bob. It felt like minutes before she dared
speak. "Are you okay?"

"You know, it's kind of funny. When I fell and broke my
arm when I was twelve, I remember my cast was so cool. All
the kids signed it and I felt so important and brave; and it's
strange, but I can't remember actually falling from the tree."
She could hear his voice start to falter, but he continued,
"Laura, I do remember him catching me when I was just
four—isn't that amazing? I still remember."

"You want to know what I think?"

"What's that?"

"I don't think the letters were written only to Emily."

"What is that supposed to mean?" Bob questioned. "Never
mind the fact that each one starts out 'Dearest Emily'?"

"I'm just telling you what I think. I know what the letters
say, but look at the things they say, at the way they are written. If this last letter isn't written directly to you, then what
is? And why are there three books and not just one? I think
he was writing to you—and Michelle. I think that if the letters had started out 'Dear Bob,' you would have discounted
them as words from your crazy old father. I think he wanted
to tell you these things directly. I think he was dying to be a
good father, to share his feelings with you—the desires of his
heart—but he couldn't. Perhaps, because of losing Kathryn,

perhaps for some other reason we can't understand—I have no idea why, but he couldn't."

"Or simply didn't."

"Perhaps, but you weren't exactly easy on him growing up, were you? I mean did you ever consider not getting along could have been as much your fault? Maybe it was a combination of both your personalities—or because men are so funny about letting their feelings show. Honestly, I don't know why you and Harry didn't talk, but I do believe these letters are his last attempt to try. Think about it, Bob. He could talk to Emily—she was his friend. By writing these letters to her, he was trying to talk to you. He was trying to have you climb up onto his knee, look into his eyes, and listen to the very best wisdom he could impart to help you get through life, to get through life better than he did. Call me crazy, but that's what I believe he intended with his *Letters for Emily*. What's more, I think you know it. I think you're starting to understand the old man, and that bothers you."

He didn't speak.

She continued, "He had his problems, Bob, no question about it. He made some bad decisions, and perhaps he wasn't always there as he should have been, but he was dealing with some pretty heavy guilt, not to mention severe depression. In his own way, he was a terrific father."

Bob simply nodded. She watched his reaction and wished she could reach into his head and read his thoughts, penetrate his façade, comprehend his anxiety. He glanced toward her briefly, then turned away to continue gazing pensively into the distance.

CHAPTER *Eighteen*

THEY WERE QUIET ON THEIR DRIVE TO THE AIRPORT AND their good-byes were awkward.

"I appreciate your sticking with me through all of this," Bob said.

"Emily's our daughter. Harry's her grandfather. What did you think I would do?" Laura replied.

"Others wouldn't have." He wasn't sure what to say next, so instead, he changed the subject. "I told Michelle we'd work something out with the will and the value of the house. It's just not worth fighting about. How do you feel about that?"

"I think that's kind, Bob. I'm sure it's the right thing to do."

He stood silently, trying to decide how best to tell her. "Listen, Laura . . ."

"Bob, if it's about us, don't—don't say any more. Just get on the plane." She was surprised at the coldness of her words as she spoke them. Bob wanted to speak, to try to explain, but the look in her eyes was devastating. He stared at her for a moment, bewildered and confused. Finally he nodded, then turned and boarded the plane.

Happy or sad, in public Laura's nature was to wear a smile. Today she couldn't and it felt strange. The last few days had been great, more than great. She and Bob had not only been civil to each other, it had almost seemed like old times. And yet if she expected, if she hoped—her heart would be broken again. She knew she could not bear it even one more time.

It was a sad moment. Not because Bob was leaving, or because things had not worked out, but rather because she understood that for the first time, she had given up hope. She had spent too many hours curled up in a ball on the closet floor with a towel held tightly over her mouth so that Emily would not hear her sob. Too many days racing to the phone when it would ring, expecting this to be the call to end her pain. Too much misery. Laura stood silent—motionless while the intercom announced the final boarding call, while people hurried by anxious to get to their destinations, while the world continued around her. It was a sad moment, an empty moment, a tearless moment. Reality had robbed her of hope.

After Emily was in bed, Laura opened Harry's book of poems and began to read. She was lonely and the book provided comfort. The emptiness she had felt at the airport remained, but with it came an assurance that she would make it. She would raise Emily the best she could on her own. She would be okay.

It didn't take long to find the next clue. "They come as gifts," she decided, "when we need them most. That must have been Harry's intention."

She moved to the computer, typed in the password, and began to read.

Dearest Emily,

Always do your best. That is all that can be asked. If at the end of each day you can look at yourself in the mirror and know that you have done all that you could do, you will live a satisfied life. I don't mean to digress again into fables, dear granddaughter, but a story related to me as a boy will serve to make a point.

There once lived a king with three sons in a faraway kingdom. He began to grow old and needed to pass on the rule of his kingdom, but he couldn't decide which of his three sons should be the next king. To solve his dilemma, he devised a contest which would test the strength and wisdom of each. On the appointed day, he gathered his sons together. These are the words that he spoke.

"Located in the distant, northernmost corner of the kingdom there stands a great mountain. It is the tallest and grandest mountain in the kingdom. Its peak stretches to the tops of the very clouds. I know this because as a youth I stood on that peak. I can tell you that at the very highest point grow some of the oldest, tallest, and strongest pine trees in the entire world. They are magnificent. To test your strength, fitness, and ability to rule, I will send each of you, one at a time, on a journey to the very highest peak of the mountain. I want you each to bring back a branch from the tallest, grandest tree on the peak. The one who brings back the greatest branch shall rule my kingdom."

And so it happened. The oldest son, sent first, headed

toward the mountain with his supplies while the king and his other sons waited. A week passed and then two. Then at the end of the third week, the young man returned to the kingdom. He had made a great effort and carried with him a huge branch. The king seemed pleased and congratulated him on a work well done.

Next it was the second son's turn. He vowed to bring even a finer branch and departed with his tents and supplies toward the mountain. A week passed and then two, and then three, while the king waited for his return; four weeks, five, and then, finally, at the end of the sixth week of his journey, the second son returned. As he approached, those watching could see he carried an enormous branch, much larger than the first. He had made a valiant effort indeed, and the king seemed ecstatic. Then, turning to his last son, he spoke. "Now it is your turn. See if you can return with a branch even larger than those of your brothers." The youngest boy's apprehension was apparent. Surely, as he was the smallest of the three brothers, he could do no better. He pleaded with his father to award the kingdom to his older brother, but the king insisted he at least try. The boy relented, and gathering up his supplies, he headed toward the mountain. Two weeks passed and then four, and six, with no word from the boy. Eight, ten, and then twelve weeks came and went. Finally at the end of the fourteenth week, word arrived that the boy had been spotted on his return to the kingdom.

In anticipation, the king commanded the entire kingdom to gather and await his son's return, for on his return he would decide who would be the future king. As the boy approached, his head was bowed with his eyes cast to the ground. He was dirty and ragged. As he neared his father, it became obvious to all that he had not even tried, for he carried no branch. Raising his eyes to meet the king's gaze, he whispered, "I have failed you, Father. My brother should be anointed king. He deserves the kingdom." As the king spoke, a hush blanketed the crowd. "Son, you didn't even try. You brought back no branch at all!" Tears of failure welled up in the boy's eyes as he spoke, "I'm sorry, Father. I didn't mean to fail you. I tried to do as you had asked. I journeyed for weeks to the northernmost tip of the kingdom, and indeed I did find a grand mountain. I climbed it as you asked, day after day, until I finally reached its very top peak, the one you spoke of visiting as a youth. I searched and searched, just as you asked. But, Father, there aren't any trees on top!"

Tears welled up now in the king's eyes as he spoke softly to his youngest son. "You are right, my boy. There are no trees on top of that great peak. Now, everything in the kingdom is yours."

Emily, always try your best—be honest, make your best effort. If you do, you will be richly rewarded in the end. I am thinking of you.

Love,
Grandpa Harry

"And we are thinking of you. Good-night, Harry," Laura whispered as she headed for bed.

CHAPTER *Nineteen*

$\mathcal{B}$OB HAD BEEN GONE FOR TWO WEEKS. HE'D CALLED ONLY once to leave a message on the machine saying that he couldn't make it out for the weekend. His tone sounded somber and she hated to call back. When she found the password to the "Joy" poem, she scribbled it on a piece of paper and faxed it to him and Michelle instead. He never called back.

It was such a beautiful letter. She called Emily down from her room and they sat on the couch to read it together.

Dearest Emily,

It's unusual to pass through life without times of sadness. They seem inevitable, often overwhelming. But God is good, and to tip the scales, to balance that sadness, he lets us experience times of pure joy as well. Watch for them. Remember them. Try to create them, if you can. No matter what, cherish them.

The moments are not the same for everyone. They often differ between men and women, even husband and wife. They may flash by, visiting only for a moment, but when they do come, life is extraordinary. Let me tell you, Emily, about the one I remember best.

It was just before Christmas, several years after we'd been married. The holidays, times of joy and celebration, were upon us when Kathryn picked up a terrible case of the stomach flu. It is miserable being sick, but at Christmas time, when there are such good things to eat, it makes the misery even worse. She loved Christmas so much, and I hated to see her bedridden on such a special day; so hoping to help, I called Dr. Worthington and made her an appointment. She'd vomited that morning, and when it came time to leave, she insisted that she felt too miserable to go out. I explained that that was the exact reason she needed to go. I bundled her up, carried her to the car, and drove her cautiously to her appointment. The office was busy when we arrived, and as was the custom in our day, I took a seat in the waiting room while she saw the doctor. I still remember the concerned look in the doctor's eyes as he stuck his head out into the waiting room and waved me to follow. Kathryn was dressed and sitting quietly on the examining room table when we entered. She looked terrible. The doctor addressed us in a solemn voice.

"I wanted you here, Harry, when I explain the problem." He was somber. "We have run several tests and at this point there is not a lot we can do about Kathryn's condition. It will no doubt worsen over the next several weeks before you see any improvement. I'll need to see her again in four weeks to check her condition."

Kathryn spoke weakly, "So, I'll be sick for Christmas?"

"Yes, I'm afraid so."

"Doc, what does she have?"

He took a deep breath and looked me in the eyes before answering. "Harry, that's why I wanted you in here next to her. I think what she has, she caught from you."

"Me? But, I feel fine." I was puzzled.

"I realize you feel fine. That's very common." His concern faded into a broad smile.

"Kathryn's pregnant, Harry."

I must admit, the news was shocking. But oh, Emily, if you could have seen Kathryn's eyes. First she laughed, then she cried, then she threw up all over the examining room table.

I implied, Emily, that I would relate to you one of my moments of joy. It may seem that I have related one of Kathryn's instead. Yet, watching her eyes, seeing her tears, feeling the energy run through her fingers as she squeezed my hand when the doctor announced the news, that moment will remain etched in my mind forever as a moment of pure delight. Watching Kathryn's happiness created a moment of joy for me.

Though she spent a good part of the morning vomiting, that Christmas turned out to be one of the most joyous Kathryn ever had. Your Aunt Michelle was born seven months later, and our life as a family had begun.

Relish the moments when they come, Emily, and share your joy as well.

Love,

Grandpa Harry

Emily was getting accustomed to the letters and didn't say much when this one was read. After a moment of reflection, she turned to Laura.

"Can I go back to my room to play?"

"Sure, honey."

Before she ran up the stairs she asked, "Did you call Dad with the password yet?"

"I sent it to him, yes."

"Did he call back?"

"Not yet. I'm sure he will. He's been very busy with his work." She seemed to accept the answer. Laura guessed Emily understood more than they'd realized. She wondered if she should tell her now. She needed to choose the right moment. After such a wonderful letter, about joy of all things, she decided perhaps it was best to wait—she would wait until Friday. If Bob didn't call by Friday, so they could decide how to tell her together, she would sit down with Emily and explain the situation to her herself. Bob would be angry, but that was life. She would take Harry's advice and climb the mountain the best she could alone.

CHAPTER *Twenty*

HE SUN WAS SHINING AS BOB RETURNED FROM THE BEACH. He wore shorts, a T-shirt, and tennis shoes, but he hadn't been jogging. He tossed his camera into the trunk next to his racket. He'd have to hurry. Brandon had beaten him badly yesterday, but today he was going to sweep the sets. He trotted back into the house, picked the pill up off the counter, and flipped it into his mouth. If he didn't hurry, he'd be late and Brandon would be ticked. Brandon was already on the court waiting when Bob arrived.

"Where have you been?"

"Sorry, I was taking pictures."

"Since when?"

"I said I was sorry. You sound like my wife."

"You look tired. Are you doing okay?"

"Better, once I kick your butt."

"That'll be a cold day in California." Brandon served, but kept up the conversation. "Speaking of your wife, have you told Laura?"

"You're just going to peck me to death, aren't you?"

"Hey, it's my job."

Bob missed the serve. He moved closer to the net and readied for the next one.

"So?" Brandon questioned again before smacking the ball.

"So, what?"

"When are you going to tell her?" He served another. This time Bob returned it perfectly. Brandon stretched but couldn't get enough force on the ball. It bounced off the top of the net. As they both approached the net, Brandon's advice turned from that of a friend to that of a doctor.

"It's time she knows what's going on. It's important."

"I've tried. I haven't been able to call her. The truth is I'm nervous."

"But you talked to Cynthia?"

"Sure, we jog together."

"You need to call Laura. Tell her everything."

"I will, I just wanted to be sure. Are the new lab results the same?"

"No change. Bob, she needs to know."

Bob knew his friend was right. After all, he was the doctor. "I'm seeing my attorney tomorrow. I'll call her afterwards," he promised.

"Deal. Now serve—if you're man enough."

Bob's palms were sweating. "You'd think I was a teenager," he muttered to himself as he picked up the phone. He tried to dial Laura's number again. On the last digit, he slammed the receiver down and swore at himself. Brandon was right, he needed to tell her everything. It wasn't fair, letting the days pass like this. Why was it so hard? What was he afraid of?

He grabbed a yellow pad from his briefcase, sat down at the table, and began to write. I guess I can understand why Harry wrote poems and letters. The thought made him laugh. Comparing himself to Harry, now that was a good one. Who would have guessed? It took a little less than an hour to get the words exactly as he wanted. Yes, writing it out was much easier, a much better idea. He tossed the finished letter into his briefcase. He was meeting with his attorney in an hour. He would give the letter to him then.

He picked up the phone and punched in Cynthia's number. "Hi, this is Bob."

"Hey, stranger. I missed you jogging."

"I know. Sorry. I had to play tennis with Brandon again this morning."

"It's getting to be a habit."

"It wouldn't be so bad if I could beat him. It's humiliating. Actually, I'm calling to let you know that I finally took your advice."

"You told her?"

"I just wrote her a letter. My attorney is sending it today."

There was an unusual silence. Bob wondered what she was thinking.

After a moment, she continued, "Bob, I don't pretend to know what the future holds, but I do think it's great you've written her. As a woman, I can tell you that she deserves to know."

"I know. That's what Brandon said. Will you be jogging tomorrow?"

"No, I think I'll give up exercise for a bit, wait to see how the storm clouds blow over first, if you know what I mean."

"I do. Until then, I guess I'll see you when I drop by Brightman's office."

"Bob, I very much look forward to it. Very much indeed."

CHAPTER *Twenty-one*

By the time Laura and Emily arrived home, the wind was getting bad, scattering dust and leaves everywhere. Laura poured Emily some milk and then trekked to the mailbox to retrieve the mail. Opening the lid was like déjà vu, a bad dream occurring over again as her fingers touched the familiar starched envelope.

"Coward," she mumbled, as she carried it inside. She tried to look cheerful as she entered the kitchen, but Emily noticed immediately.

"What is it, Mom?"

"It's a letter, honey."

"Aren't you gonna open it?"

Friday wouldn't wait. It was time she knew the whole story. "Sit down, Emily. There are some things we need to talk about."

Grabbing a knife from the drawer, she sliced the envelope open. It was from his attorney all right, but as the letter slid out, two pictures of the beach dropped onto the counter. Peculiar. Opening the folded parchment, she began to read.

Dear Mrs. Whitney:

Our client, Mr. Bob Whitney, has informed us that he will no longer be requiring our services. Unless proceedings toward a final divorce are continued through your legal counsel, we will petition the courts to drop all scheduled proceedings.

Please reply to us of your intentions within thirty days.

Also, Mr. Whitney asked if we would include the enclosed letter and photos to your attention.

Sincerely,

James Bagley

Attorney at Law

The handwritten letter on yellow stationery was clipped to the attorney's neatly typed one. Her hands trembled as she unfolded the sheet and began to read.

Dear Laura,

Over the last two weeks I've tried to dial your number several times. I could not. I found it difficult to formulate what I would say. When the words wouldn't come, I decided to try a letter. I apologize for waiting this long. Laura, there are some things you need to know. Don't be alarmed, but I have a medical condition you need to be aware of. I suffer from a depressive disorder.

The doctor has run many tests; they even took a picture of my brain, something called an FMRI, a functional magnetic resonance image. The truth is, I've wondered for a long time if

I've had a problem, but I guess I just couldn't bring myself to admit it. The day you told me about Dad's prescription, the one you faxed to me, it caused me to really question and wonder. Remember, Laura, I'm a drug rep. I knew exactly what conditions the medication treated. We also carry a similar drug for the treatment of depression. I know that such conditions are often hereditary and so just to be sure, to prove to myself that I was okay, I visited a doctor friend, Brandon Jameson. We play tennis occasionally. He's a specialist in the field. He not only ran several tests, but he also spent the better part of an hour asking me in-depth questions about my family history. Many I couldn't answer—some I could.

They concluded from all the tests that I have elevated levels of a substance called corticotropin. I know you have been doing some research into Dad's illness. You may already know what this means. If not, don't worry. It's treatable. In fact, I'm currently taking a drug that helps curb the level of the chemical the brain is overproducing. They're still fine-tuning the dosage level, but everything is going well. They told me I would probably be on medication for the rest of my life.

I've been taking it regularly and I must admit the difference is noticeable. I'm even taking pictures again. I started the medication just before coming out to search Dad's house with Greg. I wanted to tell you then, but it was too early to know. I tried to tell you at the airport, but the hurt look in your eyes was devastating. I realized then, for the first time, that I might actually be too late.

As you know, I've been enthralled by Dad's book. (Take a look at poem fifteen, by the way. Read the last six words backwards.) I find his letters fascinating. I still don't understand the contention that existed between us, but I'm beginning to reconcile myself to it. Let's just say I have gained a respect for him that I never thought I could. It was through his words, after all, that I came to know my mother.

I come now to the part of the letter I fear most. I do not intend to blame all my past actions on my condition. That wouldn't be fair. I could have done something before now. I chose not to. I had control over the way I acted and I take full responsibility for the consequences. I just want to see if I can make it right. What I am trying to say is, if you're up to trying again, I'd like to see if we can work things out. I feel so much better about the future. It's not so empty.

I never thought I would be borrowing words from my father, for in my wildest dreams I never wanted to admit that we had anything remotely in common. I'd always looked at him as just a crazy old man. I'm realizing he wasn't that crazy. He was a man struggling with life the best he could. How's that different from me?

He wrote that he was not skilled in writing, but I can think of no better way to say what is lately becoming crystal clear:

"My existence will be utterly miserable if you are not standing by my side. I will shiver, for you are my warmth—I will be lonely, for you are my friend—I will feel lost, for you are my guide. Everything good in me, no matter how small, you discover. I long to see your smile in the morning, to feel your touch in the evening."

I hope I am not too late. I will be anxiously awaiting your reply.

Love,

Bob

As Laura read the handwritten words, she was too overcome to stand. Grabbing the wall for support, she burst into tears.

"What's the matter, Mom? What does it say?"

Hugging Emily tightly, Laura spoke through her tears, "It's okay, babe, these are happy tears. Get your stuff packed. We're going to get our life back."

The wind outside was getting worse. While Emily finished packing, Laura tried again to schedule a flight at the airport. Because of high winds pushing ahead of the Pacific storm, the airlines had canceled all flights to San Diego. As a result, the remaining flights into Los Angeles and the surrounding area were overbooked. She grabbed the atlas and calculated the mileage. It would take ten hours. She would never sleep anyway. If she drove through the night, they could be there by morning.

She picked up the phone and dialed Bob's number. His machine picked up. It didn't feel right leaving her answer on his machine. She needed to give it in person. After throwing some things into her suitcase, she and Emily got in the car. Emily snuggled into her blankets in the backseat as Laura headed down the interstate in darkness.

When he noticed Laura's number on the caller ID, Bob anxiously dialed her back. No one answered. He tried her cell number. No answer. Two hours later he tried again—still nothing. To pass the time, he picked up Harry's book and began to read. Words he had once considered nonsense were now profound and meaningful.

As he turned the pages, he stopped on poem twenty-four. He read it once, then carefully again.

To Grow, We'd Garden
When I was just a little boy,
Dad took me by the hand.

Let's go work in the garden,
We'll plant the fertile land.

We'd work together often,
Dad made certain I was there.
How could I help? I was so small,
He always seemed to care.

We stood together, side by side,
Example now rings true.
Thinking back, I learned of life,
From simple things we'd do.

We'd till—I learned that good preparation is vital.
We'd plant—I learned to sow hope.
We'd talk—I learned that I was loved.
We'd fertilize—I learned to give back, not just to take.
We'd water—I learned that, as plants need water, sunshine
    and soil, we also need balance in our lives.
We'd hoe—I learned that if it is not removed, evil can soon
    choke out the good.
We'd watch—I learned patience.
We'd pray—I learned that everything in life is a blessing.
We'd thin—I learned that we all need space to expand and grow.
We'd prune—I learned that to grow the sweetest fruit, we
    sometimes need to be cut back.
We'd harvest—I learned that hard work can reap bounteous rewards.
We'd thank—I learned humility.

My dad is gone and now I'm grown,
I try to teach my son.
We spend time in the garden,
Toil beneath the shining sun.

In memory I bow my head,
And beg my own dad's pardon.
I'm not like him and though I try,
I just can't grow a garden.

It doesn't really matter though,
As a dad I understand.
I'm not here to grow a garden,
My job's to grow a man.

Of course. As Emily would say, Duh. The password was clever and yet so obvious. Harry had titled the poem "To Grow, We'd Garden." It was a play on words that fit the poem's ending perfectly. The contraction we'd was used throughout and in a poem on gardening could be read as weed. "To Grow (a) Weed Garden—very clever indeed," Bob mused.

He flipped open his laptop, typed in the password "weed," and opened the letter.

Dearest Emily,

Of all the lessons in life, the one taught here is one of the most difficult to learn, that of forgiveness. I am not speaking of forgiving others but of forgiving one's self.

I lived most of my life, Emily, full of pent-up bitterness and rage. The wounds were deep and festered for many years. They were self-inflicted wounds. Now, at the end of my time, I realize that she would have forgiven me. If Kathryn were here, she would put her loving arms around me and she would kiss me, and she would forgive me, and tell me it was okay.

Emily, in life you must face up to your actions, rectify your mistakes the best you can, and then forgive yourself and move onward.

I told you that Kathryn was taken but, Emily, her death was my fault. She left because of cruel words I spoke in a fit of anger. I pleaded with her to return. She was coming back to me when she was killed in an accident. Your father and your Aunt Michelle were not seriously hurt. Kathryn was taken. I have lived with torment every day of my life since, and now, so close to dying myself, I realize I was wrong to harbor such bitterness—she would have forgiven me.

Emily, there is no guarantee that life will be easy for anyone. We grow and learn by facing and overcoming challenges. You are here to prove yourself, to develop, and to conquer. There will be constant challenges that cause you to think, to make choices, to question. While you grow from these challenges, you will find there will be times when the day is over and you have come up short in both your actions and your intentions. Step back. Take a deep breath. Learn from your mistakes of today. Prepare the best you know how for tomorrow, and then live each day the very best you can. At the end of those days when you do come up short, my advice is to forgive yourself—forgive yourself and move on. It is how I wish I had lived my life.

I miss her, but I take comfort in the fact that she was coming back to me. I loved her with all my heart and she loved me. It is hard to explain, but I have a feeling that she will come for me soon. I look forward to being with her again.

I will miss you, Emily, but I will finally be happy. Remember me; remember your grandmother, Kathryn. We will be watching you—cheering you on.

Love,
Grandpa Harry

Bob read the words and shifted uneasily. In his mind, the words of Harry's first letter echoed: "Life has a strange way of repeating itself."

He grabbed the phone and dialed her number again. No answer. He hit a few more numbers and was instantly connected to information.

"Hi, I need a number for—let's see—his name is Grant, Grant Midgley."

He scribbled the number on the back of an envelope as it was repeated and then punched it into the phone. It rang just once before someone picked up.

"Grant Midgley."

"Hi, this is Bob Whitney, Laura's husband. Have you heard from Laura? I'm worried about her."

"Oh, hi there. Um, yes, I talked to her earlier. She called me here at home, to let me know she wouldn't be in for a few days. Said she had to take a quick trip to California to see you, work some things out. Didn't you know she was coming?"

"Not exactly. Perhaps she wanted to surprise me. Do you know what time her flight left?"

"She was driving." The words made Bob's heart sink.

"Laura, driving in this weather?"

"I guess all the flights were booked. The storm caused a bunch of cancellations, but I didn't think she was leaving until morning."

"Okay, I'll keep trying to reach her. Thanks for your time. If you do hear from her, would you give me a call?"

"Certainly." Bob recited his number and hung up the phone.

He looked at the clock and then dialed her number again. "All circuits are busy, please try your call later."

He screamed into the receiver to vent his frustration, as if the recorded voice could understand. While he paced the room, he flipped on the TV to The Weather Channel. The announcer detailed the severity of the storm that was picking up force as it moved inland. "She was never good at driving in rain," he mumbled as he clicked it off.

"Life has a strange way of repeating itself." The echo was driving him crazy. He had sworn never to be like Harry. The similarities now had him terrified. If he lost Laura, as Harry lost Kathryn, how could he forgive himself? He'd live lonely, just as Harry had lived, and then he would die lonely, just like Harry. He walked around the room again, turned on the TV, and flipped the channels rapidly before throwing the remote across the room. He wanted to run on the beach, to release his anxieties, but outside the rain was violent, as the storm's fury continued.

The window wipers were going full blast but it was still hard to see. Laura was not used to driving so long at one sitting, and in truth her eyes were beginning to burn. She thought about stopping to rest on several occasions, but the words of his letter surfaced in her mind.

". . . I will shiver, for you are my warmth—I will be lonely, for you are my friend—I will feel lost, for you are my guide. . . ."

No rain was going to keep their family apart now, she vowed. Not after all the storms that had been thrown at them over the last year. Kathryn came back and now, so would she.

Emily sat up as the thunder clapped.

"Mommy, are we going to be okay?"

"We're going to be just fine, babe. Go back to sleep. We'll be there in a couple of hours." She tried to sound calm. Each time the thunder shattered the rhythmic sound of the wipers, she gripped the wheel tighter. She couldn't let Emily know that she was terrified.

He'd stayed up all night, and he looked terrible. He rested his head on the counter, drifting in and out of a light sleep. Lights from a police car began flashing through the window. He understood their meaning, and it made him want to sob. The rain was still pounding against the windows of the house. As he squinted through the downpour, Bob could see a uniformed officer step out of the car in his driveway and run toward the front door to avoid the torrent.

The doorbell rang. He trudged toward the door, his head starting to spin. What have I done? The officer pounded sternly. Bob turned the handle and pulled the door open slowly.

Standing under the porch, but still being soaked from the blowing rain, were Laura, Emily and Officer Wayne Potter of the CHP. Bob didn't wait for an explanation. He hugged Laura tightly. Emily grabbed on to both of them as they stood crying and embracing each other.

Bob spoke first, "She didn't make it back, Laura."

"What?"

"Kathryn. She was killed on her way home." She looked into his eyes and understood the depth of his panic.

"I did make it back, Bob. I did make it back."

They embraced again as the officer shifted his weight.

"Look folks, I'm glad you're all just one big happy family, but it's raining something fierce out here and the lady's car ain't gonna get out of the ditch by itself. Now, you want me to call a tow truck or not?"

"I ran off the road a few miles up. I fell asleep. I made him bring us here before calling for a tow truck. I'm sorry."

"Let the car drown," Bob answered. "Let it drown."

Epilogue

HARRY'S BOOK HAD BEEN PLACED ON THE BACKSEAT. THEY would read it on the way.

Of the twenty-six poems, they'd solved less than half. The rest would come. There were secrets left to discover.

Bob drove the U-Haul through the cemetery gate, stopping near the south side. He stepped down, and then helped Laura and Emily out of the cab. Hand in hand, they walked to Harry's and Kathryn's graves to say good-bye. They stood quietly next to the small granite markers that lay side by side.

Bob contemplated the changes that had occurred in his life—the lessons Harry had taught him.

Laura quietly thanked Harry for helping to give back her life.

Emily missed playing checkers.

After they each paid their silent tributes, Bob reached into his pocket, pulled out the letter, and handed it to Emily. It was her idea; she knew what to do. She looked so content and happy as she bent over and placed the envelope containing Harry's last letter to Kathryn on the headstone. It lay face up for all to read. While the envelope had yellowed with age, the address still read "Kathryn Whitney, Heaven." Underneath, however, new words had been written. The words "Return to Sender—No such address"—so cruelly stamped by the post office—had been crossed out. Just below and in her best handwriting, Emily had penciled in new words, words of hope and love. The envelope now read "Kathryn Whitney—Heaven. *Hand-Delivered.*"

After she had positioned the letter in place, Laura spoke, "He'll take it to her now, babe, he knows the way." Emily beamed.

Sensing that Bob needed to be alone, Laura took Emily by the hand and headed toward the van. Bob waited until they were distant. He still had difficulty expressing his emotions. He thought back to the letter that affected him the most— the one that meant the most. He spoke softly.

"I fell out of the tree Dad, just like when I was four, and then again when I was twelve. This time, though, I was thirty-six. I needed to thank you in person, Dad, for catching me, for not letting me hit the ground. I still don't quite understand how you knew, but you were there to stop my fall. Thanks, Dad."

He walked peacefully to the van. As he climbed inside, he noticed the sun reflecting off of Emily's brown hair. Her voice was vibrant as she spoke.

"So, how long does it take to get to San Diego?"

POEMS OF *Life* BY HARRY WRIGHT

Harry Wright wrote poems to his wife and family his entire life. A few years before his death, he compiled these poems into a book, which he presented as a gift of love to his children and grandchildren—so they would remember him for the good times. That book of poems and the hidden wisdom it contains inspired *Letters for Emily.*

The irony is that it was not until well after his death that his book of poems began to rekindle memories of the true man, the man who loved life and cherished family—instead of the sick, frightened old man that he had become in those final years. Like Harry Whitney, he suffered the symptoms of aging. It also became apparent in those very late years that he struggled with mental illness; a condition he probably had most of his adult life.

I would encourage the reader to seek out the writings and letters of his or her own parents, grandparents, or other loved ones. Perhaps, in this search, hidden wisdom will be discovered as well. It may be, in reading forgotten words, in remembering their lives, their sacrifices, that their frailties will wash away, their strengths will surface, and they will be remembered fondly. *It is a wish that everyone should be granted.*

Here's to you, Grandpa—you loved life, you loved your family, and you dearly loved your lifelong sweetheart who preceded you in death. You truly were "Handsome Harry, King of the Cowboys."

MY TREASURES

The poets tell of lands afar,
Of treasures rich and rare,
Of beautied waters deep and blue
Of mounts beyond compare.

I've heard them sing of stately shrines,
Of flowers, trees so tall,
They make you stand in awe bound thought
To wonder at it all.

The trees and vales, the crystal streams
Seem they so far away,
And all the beauty of the world
To hear the rhymer say.

If I could just a poet be,
I wouldn't have to roam
To find the precious things of life,
They're safe within my home.

"Happiness Is A Child's Love"

My heart is filled with ecstasy
Because a child shows love for me;
Which makes my soul with jub'lance ring
Expressively, with joy I sing.
This love has opened wide my eyes
And now in depth can visualize
The beauty of the world about
Exhilarant, I want to shout.
My heart is filled with ecstasy
Because a child has love for me.

The magic of this child's pure love
Makes all the world like heaven above
Enshrined in spiritual majesty
With grandeur, in what 'ere I see.
The golden glow of setting sun;
Peace, when daily work is done;
And nature's creatures all about
Portray friendliness, there is no doubt.
My heart is filled with ecstasy
Because this child has love for me.

Through her I understand why He,
Said Let the children come to me.
Their love inspired Him to say
Those words that live in grace today.
Rejoicefully my life is full;
In depth becoming meaningful.
So, for her love I gratefully
Say thanks dear one, you've enhanced me.
Thus, I am filled with ecstasy
Because a child has love for me.

Grandpa - January 17, 1979

THANKSGIVING IN A FOX HOLE

As I crouch within my fox hole,
     And shells around me scream,
I'm thinking of a year ago,
     And for a moment dream
Of tables piled with steaming food,
     And people filled with cheer.
And hardly realize the change
     I've gone through in one year.

I'm praying for the day again
     When we'll together be.
And stand erect in any place,
     And know that we are free.
To know there'll be no hungry
     That granaries overflown,
And lands that now are battle scarred,
     With fertile grain be sown.

And as I wait, I meditate.
     About myself I think.
And though I'm in a fox hole
     And at the battle's brink,
I guess I, too, am thankful.
     It seems so strange, yet true,
I'm thankful that today I fight
     For liberty and you.

Harry S. Wright
Nov. 1943 or 1944

THE HUMBLER THINGS

Her life was built of humbler things,
    The joy that human kindness brings.
A glowing face in happy crowd,
    A sunset shine through golden cloud.

A song toned to a weary friend,
    Or fixing flowers she might send
Assurance when the task seemed hard,
    To those bereaved, a note, or card.

A glad hello to friend on street,
    To child a smile or sweet.
Some folk might think this way too slow
    But deepest rivers slower flow.
Yes, humble deeds more longer last
    And linger on though time may pass.

"LIFE'S PATHWAY CAN BE BRIGHT"

Along life's path the way is bright
If each will leave a little might
Of joy, for those who later tread
To help them keep their eyes ahead.

- Harry S. Wright